Change Me for My Season

by Sharel E. Gordon-Love

Giving Your Soul a Rise...One Page at a Time

ISBN-13: 978-0692236703
ISBN-10: 0692236708

PEACE IN THE STORM PUBLISHING, LLC.
P.O. Box 1152
Pocono Summit, PA 18346

Visit our Web site at
www.PeaceInTheStormPublishing.com

DEDICATION

Change Me For My Season is dedicated to the memory of my father, my fallible hero, Ronald A. Gordon. It is because of our journey through your illness that this book came to be.

To all of our African American men who have battled prostate cancer.

ACKNOWLEDGMENTS

I honor God for this writing journey He took me through that produced a work that only He could have given the blue print for ~ I am humbled.

Mom, Coretha Cobb, what can I say? You have been right by my side through so many things; your love and encouragement goes farther than words could ever express. I would not be where I am without you. I love you so much! My three sons – Khayree, my oldest son, who has grown into a wonderful, responsible young man. Thank you for having your Mom's back always; I love you! Alvin 'A.j.' Love, Jr., my middle son and the most outspoken of the three. I love your honest, no-nonsense approach to life and the stand you have taken for God. It is refreshing! I love you! Ronald A. Love, my youngest son and my father's namesake, I am so very proud of you! All that you have accomplished and those goals that will soon be realized makes me smile. I love you! To my Peanut who will be the next scholar/athlete in the family, I love you to pieces!

My Siblings! I love each and every one of you so much! My sisters: Tracey, Rhonda, Cassandra and Danielle. My brothers: Gregory, James III, Jeffrey, and Mark. Our next generation of nieces and nephews: Al-Lateef, Wafi, Janay, Tranae`, Tamara, Destiny, Takeya, James IV, Jada, Ashante, Nyia, Kanye, Arianna, Mia, and Jah'Sair! Watching God do some wonderful things in your life is priceless to me.

To my Pastor and Jurisdictional Bishop, Bishop William T. Cahoon, you are so very special to me. As I have often shared with others, there are things that you have imparted in my life that have carried me through the years. I have plenty of notebooks filled with notes from your messages that I refer to as well. I love you!

To my First Lady, R. Carolyn Cahoon; your life is a living testimony of what God can do! You are a woman of GREAT FAITH and I am thankful that you are here with us. I love you!

To Pastor Kevin D. Ginyard, Sr., once again you have shared something that was an integral part of my story. Thank you so much!

Pastor Edwin DeBourgh, you are a true friend and blessing to my life. You have encouraged me to trust God to do things that I have never done before. It's been a ride! Love you, my friend!

Much love and thanks to my New Reid Temple C.O.G.I.C. church family! Thank you all for your support.

My Peace in the Storm Publishing FAMILY! Y'all ROCK!!! I love the camaraderie we share and how we flow in God's favor. It is awesome! I love you all!

The incomparable Elissa Gabrielle (she's my publisher y'all!)! Never in a million years would I have believed I would be part of the great dynasty that God has blessed and is blessing you to build. What a legacy! I love you!

Guichard Cadet, thank you for seeing the vision with my first release, taking the time to help me hone my writing skills and to give me the first chance at becoming a published author. You are the springboard to what I love to do.

There are some special people that I hold dear to my heart. They took me under their wings when my published literary career began: Pat G'Orge-Walker, Jacquelin Thomas, Victoria Christopher Murphy, Linda Beed, Kendra Norman Bellamy,

Maurice Gray, Jr. and Shunda Brown who found me before I knew I was ready to make a public appearance.

APOOO and Yasmin Coleman and the opportunity to read great African American literature has been awesome.

Thank you to the book clubs who have featured and reviewed *The Putting Away*, particularly OOSA, Black Expressions, APOOO, VERSEDOnline and St. John's Baptist Church Sister to Sister Book Club Ministry

Remembering loved ones that helped to mold my life, my paternal grandparents, Christopher C. and Minnie M. Gordon, the importance of family and helping others. My maternal grandparents, Lawrence and Rosia Cobb, the importance of serving God. Oh, and my love for yellow cake with chocolate frosting! My Dad, Ronald A. Gordon, my shoulder and voice of reason, encourager, and hero...I miss you every single day. My step-mom, Delia M. Gordon, folks don't really know what keeping it real means unless they have ever had the pleasure of talking to you. I love and miss you! Patricia Faucette, my best friend and mentor; your wisdom lives within my heart and mind and I will never forget how you taught me by example to live for God. Bishop Ivory W. Holden, a godly man of great patience and wisdom, how blessed I am to have served under your ministry. To Sylvia Stepney, our friendship was instant and you left far too soon.

Finally, to the many readers who have stayed in touch with me and inquired about the next book. I appreciate your support and thank you for your encouragement. My prayer is that this book will bless you real good. Much love!

Seasons come and seasons go…"Change Me For My Season" by Sharel E. Gordon-Love grips the heart and plants the mind for its harvest in a literary garden of love and honesty.

~~~ Pat G'Orge-Walker, "Sister Betty Says I Do"

Transitioning Into My Change

"If a man die, shall he live again? All the days of my appointed time will I wait, till my change come." Job 14:14

February 28th – 6:30 am

"Baby, take your rest…I'll see you soon…" *I hear Tonya say as her sweet kisses flood my face. I fight with all of my might to hold on just a little while longer although I know I feel myself slipping away from what I've always known as my life.*

"Not now, Lord, not now, please?" I plead, but we settled this matter some time ago, if only I could convince Him to let me stay.

"Now, Lord? Can I see her once more, just once more?"

Struggling to open my eyes, the sight is beautiful! "Oh, I love her so much, Lord…thank you. It is done, here I am, Lord." Giving in to the peace, I close my eyes with a smile that involuntarily stretches my lips.

Chapter One

TONYA

The silence I heard when I walked in the door was over before I could make it to the den. The sound of my sons running down the stairs sounded like a stampede instead of two 17 year-old boys.

"Mom, I'm headed over to Mike's," Gary Jr. stated before I could slip my feet out of my shoes.

"Over to see Michaela," Gerald said laughing, playfully hitting his brother in the shoulder.

"Mikki to you, and I'm going to see her if I'm going to Mike's house. That's stupid, Gerald," Gary Jr. countered out of embarrassment.

"Well hello to you too, where is your sister, and what have I told you about calling each other stupid?" I asked ignoring what Gary Jr. said at first.

"The pest is upstairs," said Gerald. "Nana dropped her off after we got home since you were already on your way."

I leaned back in my chair and massaged my temples trying to put my day at school behind me and deal with what was ahead of me at home.

"I'm out, all right, Mom?" Gary Jr. addressed me again.

"Go and I want you in this house by six for dinner. Gerald,

tell Monét I said to come here, and I'm not hearing you lost track of time!" I called after the boys as they ran in different directions in preparation to leave the house.

I sat back in my comfortable easy chair and closed my eyes, not realizing I had dozed off to sleep until I felt kisses all over my face. Monét was leaning over me and had started kissing me to wake me up.

"Hi Mommy! I love you!" Monét said, kissing me one more time on my cheek.

"Hi Baby Girl... Mommy is so tired. Did you have any homework today before you turn on that TV?" I inquired, trying to muffle a yawn.

"Yes, I finished it at Nana's. Can I watch TV now?"

"I'm going to ball with Gary and Mike," Gerald quickly says as the boys pass by the den heading for the front door.

"He's the one who wants to see Mikki," Gary Jr. teases, laughing on their way out the door.

"Yeah right..."

"All I know is both of you guys had better be back in here by six for dinner or you won't be seeing Mike or his sister Mikki for a week!" I yell out only to hear a slammed door in return for my empty threat. I'd been saying that since they were little boys; it was hard to remember not to say it.

"Can I?" Monét asks, with her head tilted to the side.

"Go on and turn on the TV. I'm going to the kitchen to start dinner and just maybe I can slip in a nap," I answered, getting to my feet. Monét already tuned me out as she surfed the channels trying to decide which cartoon to watch. SpongeBob SquarePants™ was still a favorite of hers, so that's what she settled down to watch as I headed for the kitchen.

By 5:30 the smothered pork chops were finished being reheated in the oven, the mashed potatoes just needed to be whipped, left over collards from Sunday dinner was warming in another pot while I kept a watchful eye on a pot of yellow rice as I slid a pan of cornbread in the oven beside the pork chops.

Checking my watch for the time, I knew my peace would be ending in just twenty-five more minutes. The boys will be coming in, Gary will be right behind them and I still had so much to do before I could think about going to bed tonight.

"Baby Girl, wash your hands and come help me set the table," I call out to my daughter. When she doesn't come, I call her a few more times before she finally answers saying she was on her way to the bathroom. Maybe I should make her keep that TV off until after dinner because the girl acts like she can't hear a thing when it's on.

By the time Monét helps me set the table, along with serving bowls and a pitcher of iced tea, I hear the garage door open and the front door at the same time. The boys were hitting each other and laughing on their way upstairs when Gary came walking into the kitchen.

"Hey, Princess! How was school?" Gary asks Monét, taking a moment to kiss both of her cheeks.

"It was good. Do you wanna see my paper, Daddy? Nana said I did a good job." Monét said, running to get her book bag.

"Hey Babe, how was your day?" Gary asks, kissing me on the lips.

"Busy and tiring, but good... how was yours?" I ask as I skirt by him to put a small platter of butter on the table.

"Same old for the most part; I feel like I need a vacation..."

"Yeah right," I said, cutting him off. "When was the last time we went anywhere? I'm not talking about Disney either."

"You're right, we don't take time just for us, but it's coming, I promise," Gary replies, kissing me on my neck as I try to squeeze past him to put a bowl of rice on the table.

"Mmm hmmmm... I won't hold my breath."

"Why don't we plan a long weekend or..."

"Hey Dad!" Gerald interrupts when he enters the kitchen with Gary Jr. right behind him.

"Hey Fellas, what's up?" Gary says doing their special handshake with both boys.

"You're late," I said while I wash my hands at the sink.

"It was all Gerald's fault trying to get at Mikki," Gary Jr. explains.

"No, I wasn't! She was trying to tell me something if you woulda just waited for me," Gerald offered in his own defense.

"I don't want to hear it. Just make sure your hands are

washed and come to the table for dinner."

"It was Gary..." Gerald starts to explain.

"What did I say, guys? It goes for both of you and I don't want to hear another word about it," I state evenly, trying to keep my cool.

"Do what your Mom says, fellas," Gary reiterates on his way out of the kitchen to wash his hands in the bathroom.

"Mom, I'm not late for dinner, right?" Monét asks.

"Who asked you anyway, pest?" Gary Jr. said, mushing his sister upside the head.

"All right, that's enough! Sit down to the table so we can have a peaceful dinner. If anyone feels like they have to argue tonight, I'm giving your plate to Mr. Benson's dog down the street. Now have I made myself clear?" I threaten, looking at all three of my children.

Soft replies of 'yes' follow my stares as Gary makes his way back to the table. Clearing his throat, he sits down and offers grace. Once Gary finishes, we silently pass the platters, filling our plates without making direct eye contact with one another.

I knew it wouldn't be long before my husband ended the silence. He didn't have the joy of eating dinner with siblings every night, and hardly his mother, so talking was necessary.

"Your Mom and I are going on a long weekend trip soon, and you guys will stay here and Monét will stay with your grandmother," Gary said, taking a slice of cornbread from the plate in the center of table.

"With Nana Cee? Will she be checking in on us too?" Gerald asks, cutting his eyes at me. It was no secret that there was no love lost between my mother-in-law and I. "We could stay home alone without the pest," Gerald adds, giving Gary a quick look and nod.

"Sure... that is, if it's okay with your Mom," Gary adds while avoiding my eyes. "Staying home alone without some supervision is not going to happen."

"You know I don't mind," I said, not looking at anyone. I really didn't mind, it's just that I hated the fact that the relationship between my mother-in-law and I has never gone back to the way it was before me and Gary's break up years ago. If I wasn't raised to be respectful, I would have told her to go scratch by now.

"For real, Mom?" Gary Jr. dares to ask. I nod my head and my kids cheer as if they'd just won a prize...the boys because of the freedom at home, and Monét because she's going to their Nana Cee's house. I sigh and take my plate to the sink and empty it down the garbage disposal.

"Do you want me to take care of the dishes?" Gary wants to know, as I make my way back to the den and my favorite chair.

"If you want..." was all the answer I could muster up. It has always bothered me that my children prefer to stay with Gary's mother as opposed to mine. They never get excited knowing they were going to spend time at my parents' house. I'm a little jealous, but it still shouldn't be so one-sided.

Grabbing a book I started reading a week prior, I recline in my easy chair and never crack the cover open. Sleep takes over and I give into it until the wee hours of the morning when I awaken to find a blanket covering me. Instead of getting up to go upstairs to bed, I snuggle down further in the blanket and allow sleep to capture me once again. Those important things I had to do before bed had no choice but to wait.

Chapter Two

GARY SR.

I can't remember the last time I "clock watched" in all the years I've been working for BAN. There was plenty to do, and I had a few meetings scheduled later in the day, but I couldn't seem to focus on anything. The pain I've been having in my upper left thigh had me distracted, and there was no way I could concentrate long enough to get any work done. *Forget this, I'm going home*, I finally decided.

"Pamela?" I speak into the phone to my assistant.

"Yes, Gary, how can I help you?" she responds.

"Listen, I'm not feeling well, so can you clear my calendar for the rest of the day? I'm going home," I answer, leaning back in my chair.

"You must be sick… you have never gone home from work before. Do you want me to reschedule the meetings or hold off until you return?"

"Hold off for now. I'll let you know what I need you to do when I return. I'm headed out now," I tell Pamela while shutting my computer down. I was already out of my chair pulling files from the drawer to take home with me. Maybe I can concentrate better there.

"Will do! And hey… take care of yourself," concern was

evident in Pamela's voice.

"I will. I'll call you first thing in the morning to let you know if I'll be in or not," I reply as I close my brief case.

When I reached my car and got in, I sighed and leaned my head back against the headrest. I've been really tired lately, but it's probably just from working so much. Starting the car, I head towards home and look forward to hanging out in the den so I can watch TV, something I hardly ever get to do. With the kids in school and Tonya at work, I will have the whole house to myself without any interruptions.

The silence that greeted me when I opened the door leading from the garage was golden, and I hurried to take up a spot on the loveseat in the den so I could kick my shoes off and lay back with the remote control in my hand. I must have been tired because the last thing I saw was an old Divorce Court episode with Judge Mablean telling a young lady that her behavior was foolish when the phone rang, startling me from a deep sleep. I had to get my bearings before I answered the phone, almost dropping it as soon as I picked it up.

"Hello?" I answer with a sleep-filled voice.

"Gary, are you ok? I just called your office and Pamela told me you'd gone home for the day," Tonya's anxious voice fills my ear.

"Yeah, I'm um… just tired. I couldn't concentrate at work and decided I needed some peace and quiet so I can finish some things that are due on my boss's desk by the end of the week. What's going on with you?"

"Nothing… I had a break and you crossed my mind, so I called you. Are you sure you're feeling all right? Pamela sounded like maybe I should see that you go to the doctor or something," Tonya says, the worry she was trying to hide coming through in her tone.

"Baby, look, I've been working hard and I guess it's just catching up with me. Besides, when was the last time I took a day off and watched court shows on TV? I'm thinking that maybe I'll take a few days off anyway. Or we can really plan that time away that we've been talking about for so long," I tell her, trying to convince my wife that I was just tired.

"Ok, I guess we can talk about it when I get home. My break is almost up, but I'll call you when I'm on my way home. Do you need anything?"

"Just you," I answer, smiling in spite of myself.

"You've got that right!" Tonya said jokingly. "Love you, I gotta go."

"Love you too, Baby... bye," I said before putting the phone back in its place.

Leaning back on the sofa, I flipped channels while I massaged the pain in my thigh that has been bothering me for some time now. I was never one for seeing a doctor, and as long as I can go to work and take care of my family, that was most important to me. Feeling a tremor of fear travel through me, I did my best to push it away and declare out loud that it was of the enemy and my faith is whole in God. Too bad my gut kept telling me I had every reason to fear.

Later that evening after our children were in bed, Tonya wanted to sit on my lap, but as soon as she made contact with my left leg, I quickly lifted her by her waist.

"Wait, Baby, my thigh hurts..." I told Tonya, trying to keep the pain out of my voice.

"Here let me rub it for you," she offered, attempting to rub my leg just before I pulled it out of her reach.

"It aches and it feels kind of... funny... maybe I'll just soak in a tub of Epsom Salt," I said, getting to my feet to limp slowly up the stairs. How can I tell my wife that I think there is something wrong other than a pulled muscle?

Chapter Three

TONYA

Heated was an understatement! I decided not to keep trying to reason with my husband about taking care of his health. Whenever I asked him about rubbing his thigh, he would say he must have pulled a muscle. I wanted to scream! Taking a few cleansing breaths as I watched Gary getting ready for work, I decided to try again and choose my words carefully.

"Baby, I can call our family doctor and make an appointment and get you in after work. I really think you need to have your leg checked out. You've been rubbing on it for over a month and…"

"Tonya, really? I have too much to do and you know I don't go for that doctor stuff. I trust God to keep me healthy and it's like I told you before, I pulled this muscle playing ball."

"You know what? I'm making that appointment for a late night and you're going if I have to come to your office and drag you out of there! I trust God for our health too, but the doctors are not here just because they earned a degree. "

When Gary continued to dress and ignore me, I reiterated my statement and left him to prepare for work. On his way to the garage, he stopped in the kitchen and attempted to kiss my cheek, but I moved.

"Tonya, come on, don't do this."

"You're the one who is doing *this*. I want my husband here to help me raise these three children he gave me, and if taking care of your health is going to ensure that happens, then to the doctor you will go. Dr. Walters will refer you to another doctor, like an orthopedic specialist, if it is a pulled muscle. Why won't you go?"

Gary didn't answer at first, but the look on his face told me he feared something.

"What is it?"

"It's nothing…listen, go ahead and make the appointment. I have a feeling this conversation will not go away until I do." Kissing me quickly on my cheek, Gary headed out and then turned back to me. "This is for you, hear?" he asked, walking back to me. "When I do it, I don't want to hear about it again for another twenty years, got it?" Before I could answer, Gary pulled me into a hug and kissed me full on the lips until we were interrupted by the boys.

"Man, I knew they were kissing," Gerald commented.

"Don't worry fellas, you will find a girl just like your Mom and you will want to kiss her all the time too," Gary told our sons.

The boys looked at each other and burst out laughing, giving each other daps. All I could do was shake my head and send my husband out the door with another kiss and a prayer that he would actually go to the doctor once I make the appointment.

After fussing at the boys and making sure Monét had all of her things in her book bag, we each headed to our destinations for the day. Monét attended the middle school in our neighborhood, having entered the 6th grade, the boys are at the end of their junior year at Stoney Brook High School, which is in walking distance, and I teach 5th grade at a school across town.

I did not forget that I told Gary I would be making an appointment for him to see our family physician. I knew that a pulled muscle could not last for weeks on end, and if it did, it had to be something like a torn ligament. Running different causes through my mind didn't help, and waiting for my break seemed to take longer than usual. As soon as the bell rang for lunch to begin, I headed to my car, pulling out my cell phone as

I walked.

Making an appointment was not easy at first, but I convinced the receptionist that my husband needed to see Dr. Walters as quickly as possible. Finally after 15 minutes, she came back to the phone to tell me that Gary could see the doctor at six this evening or nine the following morning. I made the appointment for tonight because we needed to get to the bottom of Gary's problem as soon as possible.

Pushing the end button on my cell, I immediately scrolled through my contacts for Gary's cell, hoping he would pick right up. Instead of ringing, it went straight to his voicemail, so I called Gary's office, tapping my fingers waiting for him to answer. Five rings later, Pamela answered, and I told her to inform my husband that he had a doctor's appointment and the time and he'd better pray that I won't have to come and get him myself

"I will tell him, Tonya. I've been worried about that limp that he says is nothing, but it's obvious he's in a lot of pain," Pamela told me.

"You're right, and we're going to get to the bottom of it now because I'm tired of his 'pulled muscle' excuse," I shared.

"Gary doesn't have any meetings past three today, so maybe he will leave a little early for a change."

"If he doesn't want me at his office, he'd better meet me at home by four. Please tell him that for me, will you, Pam?"

"I certainly will! Have a good rest of the day, Tonya."

"You too!"

Making Gary's appointment did not give me the relief I expected, but at least he would be going. Praying the rest of the afternoon in between history and math consumed me and exhausted me by the end of the day. I was so relieved when the dismissal bell rang and I walked my children out the door. Instead of heading back to my class like I normally did, I prepared by packing my things so I would be able to head straight to my car once the last student left for the day.

The first thing I did once I got into the car was to pull out my cell phone to see if I had a message from Gary. I knew my husband well, because I really didn't expect a voicemail from him confirming his appointment. Immediately I called his cell and waited for him to answer. Just before it was about to go to voicemail, Gary answered.

"Hey, Sweetheart, I'm headed home now. I had an un-scheduled meeting later in the day and it couldn't be helped. Where are you?"

"I'm headed home, too," I answered chuckling, because Gary knew he'd better be going in the same direction that I was going.

"Okay, I'll see you there."

The next call was to my mother asking her to keep Monét until I picked her up, explaining all that I had to do, but a feeling of dread refused to leave the pit of my stomach. I decided that if I didn't give voice to it, it would stay just a feeling. No need to be anxious about something that did not happen.

Once Dr. Walters examined Gary, he invited us into his office to talk to us together. When I saw the fear in Gary's eyes, the feeling of dread returned to the pit of my stomach with a vengeance. Wanting to ask Gary what the doctor told him was on the tip of my tongue, but I decided to wait to see what the he wanted to tell us. I grabbed my husband's hand to reassure him and to keep myself from bursting into tears. I couldn't imagine my strong husband having to deal with any kind of illness, but the serious look we were receiving from our doctor when he usually smiled brightly, caused the dread to travel to my chest.

"Gary, I will be straight with you...your prostate is en-larged, and the halting urination is caused by the narrowing of your urethra tube by what could be a tumor. Now, it can be caused by something other than prostate cancer, like a disease called benign prostatic hyperplasia, or BPH...it's a non-cancer-ous increase in the size of and the number of cells that make up the prostate."

"Is that what you think it is?" I asked, my voice trembling.

"We won't know until we run some tests, starting with a prostate specific antigen blood test, which is also used to help diagnose prostate cancer," Dr. Walters explained.

"Will you be sending me for these tests?" Gary asked in a low voice.

"Actually, what I want to do in order to move ahead quickly, is to send you to an urologist from here so that any tests you need can be ordered by the specialist. Then once the tests come back, if need be, he will refer you to an oncologist."

"What about the pain in his thigh? Gary has been complaining about it for a couple of weeks now, and it has not gotten any better."

"Gary?"

"Baby, I…it's not just my thigh, it's my leg period. I just didn't want you to worry…"

"Gary! Are you kidding me? I've been trying to believe…" and immediately my tears cut off my voice and I left Dr. Walters's office headed for the car. I couldn't take another word of what I was hearing, and I was thankful Gary didn't try to get me to come back inside.

Needless to say, there was no conversation going on in the car as Gary drove towards our home. I was seething! It was better that we didn't talk; opening my mouth would have only released the scream that was burning in my chest. How could he do this to me? Unbelievable!

"Do you want to stop for coffee before we go home?" Gary asked, not taking his eyes off of the road for a second to look at me.

Instead of answering him, I turned the radio on and he got the message. I didn't want him to stop anywhere, just take me home so I could process this stuff in silence. I could feel the heat of my anger burning me up from the inside out, and I could not for the life of me understand why my husband of almost 18 years decided that he didn't need to tell me the truth about how he was feeling. Why?

Once the garage door closed, I opened my car door and headed for the door leading into the house.

"Tonya, Baby, wait a minute…"

"No! I can't do this right now, Gary," I answered with a new round of tears hurting my eyes.

"Please, Tonya. I want to tell you why I didn't tell you."

Stopping just before entering the door, I refused to turn

around to face my husband because if his reasons for not telling me were not good, I was afraid I would hit him to rid myself of the anger that refused to budge.

"Tonya..."

"Go ahead and say it or you won't have a chance again," I threatened through clenched teeth, tears chasing each other down my face.

"I'm scared...okay? I'm scared and...and...I don't need both of us to be afraid at the same time. I need you to be my rock like you always are, and I didn't want to see you hurting..."

Silence filled the space between us as my husband's words began to leave my ears and mind to trickle to my heart where I acknowledged the fear that I'd seen in his eyes for the last few weeks. I turned to embrace my husband and wailed, a cry that brought the boys to the garage. Before they could ask what was wrong, Gary told them to go back inside.

"But, Dad..."

"Back inside fellas, I have your Mom. Go ahead, she'll be alright in a minute, just go."

Reluctantly, the boys obeyed their father, but not without looking back at me a few times before finally going back inside. How in the world are we going to tell our children about their father's health?

Chapter Four

GARY SR.

It was hard getting my wife to calm down enough to face our sons who were waiting for us in the kitchen once we made it inside the house. They looked at each other and then looked to both Tonya and I to start talking. I knew that Tonya would not do it, so I sat down at the kitchen table to let them know that I would be going through some things while she made her exit. I prayed they did not sense my fear, or see it anywhere on my face.

"So, Dad, what does all of that stuff mean?" Gerald asked once I repeated what Dr. Walters told my wife and me a few hours earlier.

"It means that I have to stay on top of my health better, that's all. I will be going for further tests and then, more than likely, some medication to fix what has gone wrong. Over time, the condition will improve and all will be well," I attempted to explain to my sons.

"Why was Mom crying like that? We thought you hurt her or something," Gary Jr. stated, narrowing his eyes at me.

"I would never intentionally hurt your mother, so stop looking at me like you could get at me, because that would never happen either. You hear me?"

"Well, we're old enough to protect Mom now…"

"And I've always been here to provide the protection she needs, so watch it, Son. Don't start feeling yourself because you got some height and weight on you. Understood?" When Gary Jr. did not respond, I asked once more, "Understood?"

"Yeah…I mean yes, Dad."

"We're done here; if there's more to tell you once all of the testing is done, your mother and I will let you know."

As I watched my sons get up and walk out of the kitchen, I saw replicas of myself and realized that my son spoke the truth about protecting their mother. Gary Jr. and Gerald were both about two inches above my six feet, the evidence of their impending manhood showed in their muscle-defined bodies. It amazed me that I would have children that looked so much like me that it was scary, yet I could feel my chest puffing up of its own volition remembering their accomplishments.

Gerald has always been the book worm, intrigued by science and math, making sure he kept his grades at an "A" average, while Gary Jr. skated between "B's" and "C's" with a steady "A" in gym. Both boys enjoyed basketball, but Gary Jr. preferred football over basketball since I allowed them to play with Pop Warner when they were growing up.

Sighing heavily, I went in search of my wife to see if she was feeling better about what we were about to face. For the most part it was the unknown I was most concerned about, but I needed to assure Tonya that everything was going to be all right. Perhaps if I could steady the slight tremor of fear that coursed through my body right under my skin, I would be able to give my wife the reassurance she needed.

Entering our bedroom, I could see that Tonya had removed her clothing and saw that the light was on in the bathroom, but when I tried the door, it was locked. Trying to decide if I should knock on the door, my mind was made up for me when I heard my wife crying from her soul. I couldn't bring myself to bother her, so I laid across the bed to wait for her to come out of the bathroom. I knew it would be some time before she would when I heard the water in the bathtub and smelled the scent of Tonya's favorite Victoria Secret's cherry blossom seeping from under the door.

When I opened my eyes an hour later, my wife was apply-
ing lotion to her beautiful legs with her back to me. The urge to
touch her in some way would not be squelched, so reaching out,
I allowed my fingertips to graze the side of Tonya's right arm
and she flinched, but never stopped putting lotion on her body.

Getting up, I walked around to face her; getting on my
knees, I stilled her hands and looked into the eyes of the woman
I've loved since high school. It was not long before the tears I
knew Tonya was fighting coursed down her cheeks quickly.

"Baby, please don't cry, everything is going to be okay," I
said, pulling Tonya into a tight embrace. Her response was to
cry even harder, but as much as I felt helpless, I refused to let her
go. Holding on to my wife helped me to at least feel like I was
being strong for her because I was finding it hard to be strong
for myself.

We stayed in our embrace for close to twenty minutes before we could finally break apart to look into each other's eyes.
I was afraid to speak for fear that my true feelings would re-
sound in my voice, so I waited on Tonya, the true strength of
our family, to say something first. Instead of talking, she placed
her right hand on the left side of my face and caressed it as if it
were the first time she ever touched it. With a quick kiss to my
lips, Tonya got up and finished dressing for bed, while I sat and
watched her before going to the bathroom to take a shower. I
was hoping the feeling of defeat that I was wearing like a coat
would wash off and down the drain. Unfortunately it followed
me to bed as I lay holding Tonya in my arms, listening to her
taking deep breaths in between the tears that would not stop
falling from her eyes.

The following morning, it was business as usual in the
Simmons' household; the guys running back and forth up and
down the stairs trying to make sure they had everything for
school, saying they were glad their sister stayed at Tonya's parents' house last night knowing full well they missed their daily
tease fest. Tonya was fussing at them to make sure they ate
breakfast while I was in the bathroom shaving. I really wanted

to sit in my bedroom and listen to the sounds of life in our home, but I was running a little late myself and needed to get a move on.

Heading into the kitchen to grab a couple of pieces of toast and wish my family well for the day, I decided being late would have to suffice. I wanted to sit at the table with Tonya and try to talk to her about what we will have to do soon, and I didn't want to leave the house until then.

"Are you okay this morning?" Tonya asked, not turning to face me.

"Yes...do you have a minute?"

"I have to get over to my parents' house to get Monét to school and then I've got to go to work, you know that."

"Look at me please, Tonya...can you look at me?"

"Gary, let's not start something we can't finish. Why didn't you get up earlier if you wanted to talk?"

Getting up from my seat, I grab my wife and turn her to face me. "Listen, I know you're still upset with me, but don't shut me out...I need you..."

Instead of answering me, Tonya wraps her hands around my neck, caresses the back of my head and then kisses me ever so sweetly on the lips and whispers in my ear, "I love you... now let's go to work." Letting me go, she playfully whacks me on the butt and hollers for the boys to get it in gear. The first genuine smile parted my face and I grabbed my keys and headed for the door feeling a little lighter than I did just moments prior. Yes, everything is going to be just fine. That is, until I walked through the door of my office.

Nothing with the new project we were working on was going right, and my feelings about our new Director was confirmed when he literally ran into my office trying to explain what he did and what he figured I could fix for him.

"What I did was implement part of the system I learned at my previous job and figured since they were similar, it would work together seamlessly," Dan tried to explain while running his hands through his thinning pate.

"Why don't you sit down and tell me exactly what you

did. It sounds like we will have to take the system down and remove the parts you implemented and redo everything from the top. Let the team know that the system will be down at least for the next 48 to 72 hours while we work," I advised. That's what happens when you pass over a qualified person to hire who you wanted.

Dan's face became redder when he informed me that he asked the team to undo what he did. I dropped my head and took a deep breath before telling him I would take care of it.

"What should I be doing?" Dan inquired with a sheepish look on his face.

"How about calling the client and let them know that their system will be up and ready to go at the end of the week. Tell them we found something that would cause them problems down the road, and we wanted to ensure that it didn't…because surely this will," I said, looking into the program Dan decided to take over and mess up.

Looking relieved, Dan thanked me and started out of my office. Pausing before opening the door, he asked, "This is between you and me, right Gar?"

"Gary," I reminded him. "Yes, we don't have to tell anyone what's being done. Just re-route some duties for the team and I'll do what I can to fix this. Ask Pamela to come into my office on your way out," I stated, waving him on without looking up from the program I opened.

Minutes later Pamela knocked on my office door before entering.

"Hey, Boss, everything okay?"

"Not at all, but I need to go over my calendar for the remainder of the week and reschedule a few meetings and get ready to put in a little over time. My wife is going to kill me, so get your black dress ready," I commented, making a bad attempt at a joke.

Chuckling, Pamela said, "I hope she doesn't because it looks like it's going to take half the day to get the team going on something else while you do this."

"Tell me about it."

After Pamela helped me rearrange my calendar and get the

team together to undo the mess that Dan created so the higher ups won't end up in an uproar, I decided to take an early lunch and head across town to the school where Tonya teaches. It's been a long time since I've surprised her, so I decided to pick up a grilled chicken salad with French dressing on my way. I had to find a way to help ease my wife's fears if I was going to make it through the testing phase with the doctor.

Before I could knock on her classroom door, a few of the kids could see the flowers I decided to pick up through the window and blew my surprise.

"Ooooooooh, Mrs. Simmons, your boyfriend is at the door!" a little girl with a head full of braids and as many barrettes said, while pointing in my direction.

"Girl, whatchu know about a boyfriend? Your momma don't even let you out the house after dark," a tall lanky boy commented, followed by laughs and more teasing.

"Class, that's enough, quiet down! Begin reading in your history books where I just told you and I will be right back," Tonya told her class as she made her way to the door.

"Hey Baby…"

"Gary, you are disrupting my class," Tonya whispered through clenched teeth.

Taken back a bit, I waited a beat to respond. "I wanted to surprise you…spend lunch with my wife?"

"You're just a bit too early, ok? How much time do you have?"

"As much as I want right now," I said, attempting a smile that would not fully form.

"Tell you what, stay here and let me see if I can get someone to watch my class and I'll meet you at your car. Maybe 15 minutes from now?

"Yeah, okay…" I answered, already walking away with my head down just a notch. Tonya is driving me crazy because I know she's avoiding our conversation as much as I needed it.

Fifteen minutes turned into thirty when Tonya finally made it to the car. I was about to start the car when she opened the passenger door and slipped in, apologizing for taking so long.

"So what do you have for me?" she asked, peeking into the

bag on the console.

"Baby, wait before you dig in, we need to talk."

"Not trying to be insensitive, but I'm hungry and I don't have a lot of time before I have to be back in the classroom… can't this wait until tonight," Tonya wanted to know just before she put a forkful of salad into her mouth.

"Why don't you tell them you have an emergency and you have to leave and we can go hang out in the park, or…"

"You know I can't do that, Gary. Although, I have to say it's definitely something we could plan to do, just another day. Ok?"

I looked out the window on the driver's side, hunched my shoulders and said, "Sure…whatever…"

"I've got to go in a few minutes…"

"So you're just going to go back inside without talking to me?" I quickly asked, cutting Tonya off. Now I was getting angry and I could feel my nostrils flaring.

With her fork frozen in mid-air, Tonya squinted her eyes and moved closer to me. "I just know you're not getting mad with me. I had no idea you were coming by today, but I do appreciate the lunch since nothing looked good on the cafeteria menu today," my wife chuckled.

After I started the car, I reached over and closed the container the salad was in and told Tonya she could go ahead back inside. "Sorry to impose on your time," I sulked.

"Awww, my big ole baby, put your lip in…" Tonya soothed, but when she turned my head towards her, the tears I could no longer fight welled up in my eyes. "Baby, what's wrong?"

Composing myself, the only words I could get around the rock in my throat was, "I'm scared." If I couldn't tell anyone else, I knew that I had to let my wife know how I was feeling in order to push through the expected testing and results.

"Gary, I'm here with you every step of the way. I'm scared too, but I'm believing God to take us through victoriously… don't you?"

"Yes, but…I mean, it's different when you're the one going through something like…like…"

"Cancer. I get it, Baby, I do. I never thought it would hit

us this close to home, but we know that we belong to God, and we're not claiming the worse. With that in mind, remember we are more than conquerors."

Instead of being able to suck up my tears, I ended up burying my head in my wife's chest and cried like I have never cried before. I didn't feel an ounce of embarrassment while the heavy sobs took my breath away, leaving me weak physically and emotionally. Once I was able to get myself together, Tonya took the napkin she was holding and wiped my face, followed up by a kiss each time.

"We're going to be all right…it's just a process, it's a test, and we will make it through to the other side. You never know why God has us in this place, but it's all for His glory," Tonya continued to encourage. Her smile lifted my spirits and her words the salve I needed to regain my strength and my faith.

"Thank you, Sweetheart, I don't know what I would do without you," I expressed, leaning in to kiss her real good. "You'd better get back inside."

"You sure you're ok?" Tonya wanted to know, looking into my eyes.

"I'm good now," I told her while I helped her pack up her lunch. Tonya leaned over to kiss me once more before she left the car, and I watched my wife in that beautiful dark blue dress and black three-inch pumps as she walked back into the building causing me to become more than a little warm all over.

Chapter Five

TONYA

Summer swiftly showed up, but it did not slow my boys down when it came to playing basketball or football and hanging out with friends. Monét decided that she wanted to take dance, so my days were filled with that and standing with my husband as he went through the testing ordered by the urologist who ultimately referred him to an oncologist.

Changes in my husband's physical stamina had me a little concerned since he has always been an energy dynamo. I tried to relax while I sat in the waiting room in Dr. Weiss's office for Gary to return from the examining room. Picking up a few pamphlets, the first thing I read was "One out of Six men in America have prostate cancer." *Not my husband, I'm not claiming a thing!"* I thought to myself. *Humph, not even gonna claim it!* Yet there was this nagging feeling I kept getting in the pit of my stomach that was more dread than optimism. Reading further, I felt a little better because it said, "In fact, prostate cancer is the second most deadly cancer for men in America. And it's the leading cause of cancer-related death in men over age 75." Gary's in his 40s, so perhaps this will all be over and we can go back to the chaos of normal that is our lives.

Instead of Gary coming back out so we could go home, he motioned for me to come back to the doctor's office with him so that I could hear what Dr. Weiss had to say to him. My thoughts were that it would be better coming once from the doctor without me having to decipher what was going on with a man who is not big on details.

Sitting down in front of Dr. Weiss, I could not tell whether Gary was really sick or it was something as simple as Dr. Walters had shared with us previously. But once he pulled papers from Gary's file, the doctor's wrinkled forehead told me he suspected something was definitely wrong.

"Mr. and Mrs. Simmons, overall Gary's tests look good with the exception of the PSA or the prostate specific antigen blood test. His level is higher than 4.0 ng/mL, which can be an indicator that cancer is present in the prostate. However, there are men who have tested higher and only had a urinary tract infection or prostatitis, which is inflammation of the prostate, but we've ruled both out. Since we know the prostate is enlarged, and I do feel something there, what I would like to do is a biopsy and then begin moving from there."

"I mean, you just put it out there and wait for your patients to digest it without chewing it, don't you?" I remarked. Gary looked like the wind was kicked out of him, so I took over the conversation and questioning.

"So this biopsy is done in the hospital?"

"Oh yes, most definitely. We could do it here, but I feel most comfortable in the hospital environment," Dr. Weiss explained, while unconsciously patting the top of his graying thinning pate. "My receptionist will give you the information concerning the testing, and she will set it up for you. Just follow any directions you are given before you arrive. It's a one-day procedure, so you will go home the same day."

"Are you actually cutting the prostate open to get to it, or just how is this done?" I wanted to know.

"Well, there are three procedures that can be done…transrectal, transurethral, and transperineal. Our urologist will perform the biopsy, and he usually prefers to perform the transrectal biopsy, which requires that he insert a thin ultrasound probe into the rectum so that he can identify the area that has to be anesthetized. This also helps to guide the biopsy device, and once everything is in place, a hollow spring-propelled needle will be used to retrieve thin cylindrical sections of tissue…"

"Cylindrical? How much pain am I going to be in?" Gary asked, finally finding his voice.

"Yes, tube-shaped tissue that will be tested; and as for pain, you will feel discomfort during the procedure, maybe a little soreness and light bleeding from the rectum afterwards. You may even see a little blood in your urine and/or stools for a few days as well, but it will go away. Oh, and your semen may appear to be red or rust-colored, so don't be alarmed. I will give you a prescription for antibiotics that I want you to take for a few days after the procedure to ward off infection."

"What if I decide I don't want this biopsy done?" Gary inquired.

"Oh no, you are going to have the testing done because we have come too far with this to just stop before we really find out what is going on with you. I'd rather we know what we're dealing with than to live in the dark, holding our breath everyday wondering if something is going to fall off," I pushed. "Go ahead, Dr. Weiss; is there anything else you want to add to this?"

Smiling, Dr. Weiss told us that he wanted Gary to have his receptionist set up the testing stating he will not ask us to make an appointment to get the results, he will call Gary directly. That way he will only make an appointment based on the results of the test.

Shaking hands with the doctor, we headed out to the reception area to make the necessary appointment and then decided to take a long ride back to the house, holding hands like we did in high school. No words were shared between us, but the comfortable silence seemed to be just what we needed before we went home to the questioning eyes of our three children.

The following week shattered our lives in ways I could never explain…Dr. Weiss waited until the evening to call to tell us that Gary does indeed have prostate cancer. He would have to remove the diseased prostate and find out during surgery and other tests to determine if the cancer has spread to the lymph nodes or other areas of Gary's body. Dr. Weiss wanted to see us in his office to talk further about the surgery itself that will include a pelvic lymphadenectomy. In the meantime, a CAT scan and MRI must be done to determine whether it has spread to the bones or anywhere else in Gary's body and to determine the course of treatment once that is done. My body was in too much pain to cry, and my heart felt like it was beating on speed, which started a headache across my forehead forcing me to seek refuge in our bedroom. There were no words of comfort I could offer Gary right now when I needed to be comforted as well.

I never heard Gary come to bed, and I would have questioned it had I not seen the crumpled sheets on his side, evident that sleep did not visit him. Somehow or other, I was able to escape through slumber, but something told me that being able to rest in the Simmons' household was going to be far and in between for quite some time.

Summers were easier, so by the time I had gone down to the kitchen, my children had fixed their own breakfast and was making plans to leave the house in some way. I sat at the table with a cup of tea trying to make sense of everything that turned our world upside down, and how we would tell our children what was going on without them worrying too. All that would escape me were sighs and more sighs, praying wasn't even on my mind.

"Hey, Mom, I'm going to take my graduation pics," Gerald said, kissing me on my right cheek.

"Are you and Gary going together?"

"Gary's appointment isn't until tomorrow, so he'll probably get a pick-up game with the fellas or something," Gerald shared as he grabbed a bottle of water from the refrigerator.

"What are your plans for the rest of the day?"

Shrugging, Gerald said, "Not sure...I need to check out some more colleges to see where I want to go. Plus we have to start thinking about financial aid and..."

"Hold on, take it easy...you still have a little time to worry about the financial aid. Besides, we have a little something put away for you all, so don't get too ahead of me and your father. We want to be a part of your journey," I told Gerald, playfully tapping him on his left arm.

"I hear you, Mom, but you know I have to know what I'm doing with as much detail as possible."

"Right, until I ask you to explain why you did something you shouldn't have and then you get all speechless on your mother," I smiled at my handsome son.

"True…but I can't tell you everything," he said, ducking to miss my next hit. "Be back soon, okay?"

"Where's Monét?"

"Out front talking to her friend Dana. Do you want me to call her in?"

"No, Baby, she's okay out there."

After being left to my thoughts, I couldn't help wondering how my children's lives would be changed and how they would each react to the news that their father has cancer. Gary and I haven't talked about it, but I'd rather wait until his appointment with the doctor so we will know what to expect before trying to explain things without all the answers.

"I need to talk to my girls," I said aloud to the kitchen walls. Sending a text to Lisa and Denise, I sat sipping my luke-warm tea awaiting a response. Instead of returning the text, Lisa called me. Our conversation was brief, and I told her I'd text her once I heard from Denise so we will know what time to Skype. That is the only way I was going to have this conversation with my girls. I hope they're ready for the bomb I'm about to drop on them.

~~~~~~~~~

It was 8 o'clock in the evening by the time all three of us were able to get on Skype…Lisa had the youngest children, but Brian was home and I was able to slip away to Gary's office for privacy. No need for my children to overhear our conversation before we're ready to tell them what was going on.

"Let me tell you, I've been going to church with my Mom, and I kinda like it and the bass player," Denise laughed. "He's young though, so I'm going to flirt with him until I find some-body my age that's all up in the church."

"You need a husband so you can finally calm yourself down," Lisa said, trying not to join in on the laughter.

"Right, and then what am I supposed to do when I get tired of him? Cause you know I will."

"So what's new in your world, Tonya? You haven't said much and you asked for this virtual girl's night out," Denise pointed out.

"I know, right? Well, what I have to tell you is not easy and I don't want you to say anything to anyone else, do you hear me? It's a private matter and my children don't know yet, nobody else knows but Gary and myself..."

"Spill it already!" Denise shouted, pushing her face closer to the screen. "Don't let me find out you and Gary got another baby in the oven, we're too old for that."

"I wish it were something as wonderful as the birth of a baby, but...I'll just say it...Gary has prostate cancer."

Denise audibly gasped and Lisa's eyes were so wide, I thought they were going to merge across the bridge of her nose, and that's when the tears began to fall. In between deep cleansing breaths, I told my girls what I would never tell my husband, "I'm so afraid that I'm going to lose my husband..."

"Nuh uh, no you're not, Sweetie, no you're not; there is too much available now to treat cancer, and they have made strides..."

"But we don't know what stage it is yet, Lisa..."

"Has it spread to the lymph nodes?" Lisa wanted to know.

I shrugged my shoulders and sighed deeply, wiping my eyes, searching for a tissue to clean my nose.

"Well then, you should be confident that they found it early and Gary will have a full recovery...right?"

When I was finally able to speak again, I told Lisa, "The doctor won't be able to tell us anything until he runs a few more tests and Gary has surgery. But when my husband is afraid, it's hard for me to keep pretending that I'm as strong as he believes I am."

"But y'all believe God will bring him through, so I know Gary's going to be okay," Denise finally found her voice. "The Gary I know is a fighter, and I know that your faith is going to take you through. You just make sure you keep me and Lisa in the loop and don't worry if you have to call me late at night or the wee hours of the morning, just call. Now you know Lisa don't have that testimony 'cause Brian will have that…"

"Denise! Really?"

"Tonya, you know it's the truth, and I was only going to say her butt. I've been working on this potty mouth I picked up since I moved to Georgia," Denise smiled, showing us all of her teeth.

"Denise is right, we're here for you. Is it okay if I tell Brian? He's a doctor and he understands the need to keep the information to himself. He will be here to answer any questions you may have, if you want him to."

"It's amazing to me how our primary care physician can run all this stuff down, but because it's not his specialty, we were referred from one doctor to another. Gary didn't complain about being in pain or any other side-effects from the biopsy, but I know he was having some discomfort. He hasn't said a word to me about the diagnosis, and he left this morning without waking me. I'm really worried about him."

"You know men don't talk, Girl," Lisa reminded me. "When he's ready, he'll share. I just hope your guys will be all right once they hear the news. I'm worried about Monét even more."

"I'm going to suggest we wait until we know the treatment process and expectations before we tell them. I can't be strong for all of us," I lamented.

Silence took up the space of our conversation for a solid three minutes before Denise decided she wanted to show Lisa and I her bonus check she earned from her job, and asking us to help her decide on her next big purchase. It must be nice to have a son graduating college and only having to worry about herself.

"Ladies, I hear the garage door opening and that means my hubby has made his way in from the office. I've got to go, so until next time, muah, muah!"

"Okay Tonya, just keep us posted please. I've got to go and get BJ ready for his bath and the bed. That boy finds dirt where there is none."

"You know I know about dirt with the twins. Take care!"

"Yeah, and kiss them babies for me. Tonya's kids done got

too grown for Auntie Denise's kisses."

"I don't know, Denise; when you see Gary and Gerald again, you will be quite surprised. Have a good night, Ladies, I love you both…"

Before I could log off of the computer, I heard Gary coming down the steps calling my name. I quickly walked into the laundry room and pretended to be doing something in there so Gary would not ask me about coming from his office.

"Hey, Baby, how was your day?" Gary asked, kissing me lightly on the lips.

"Ok, I guess. I didn't really do much of anything, but Gerald went to take his graduation pictures. I can't wait to see the proofs."

"Yeah…what's for dinner? I'm starved."

"Food," I said, slipping around Gary to head back up to the kitchen. But when I heard Gary coming up close behind me, I took off running only to be caught just before I reached the top step.

"Oh, you thought you could outrun me, did you?" Gary teasingly asked, as he held me in his arms and began kissing my face and my neck.

"You're not going to get any dinner if you don't quit… stop!" I laughed, enjoying this intimate time, albeit brief, with my husband.

"You win, but it's on after the lights go out tonight," Gary threatened me, swatting me on the butt once he allowed me to continue into the kitchen.

~~~~~~~~

The next two weeks went by swiftly, and it was hard keeping things from our children, but Gary agreed that we shouldn't say anything until we knew what exactly we were dealing with and the process. Once the bone scan and MRI was done, surgery was scheduled to remove the prostate, and that's when talking to our children was harder than it was when I called myself telling my sons about girls.

On the way home from Dr. Weiss's office, Gary asked if we could stop at my parents' house to share with them what is going to transpire in the coming weeks. As soon as we walked through the front door, the first thing my mother asked was, "What's wrong?"

Looking at each other, Gary and I told them we needed to share with them what the doctor told us and what we are going to have to deal with going forward.

"Lord have mercy..." my mother whispered, with tears in her eyes.

"Are they sure it's in the third stage?" my father asked right behind my mother.

"From what they can see, it has not spread, at least not anywhere else in my body," Gary explained, trying to sound more optimistic than he was.

"When are they going to perform the surgery? I'm going into prayer about this thing," my mother decided, getting up from her seat to place her arms around Gary. "It just doesn't sit right in my spirit."

An uneasiness settled around us, each of us occupied by our own thoughts until my father asked Gary to go with him into the kitchen. Once they left my mother and me in the den, I found myself wrapped in my mother's arms, something I didn't realize how much I needed until then.

"Sweetheart, what is the doctor really saying? Gary isn't..."

"No, Mom, but it's been hard keeping up this brave front for him. They won't really know what his true prognosis is until after the surgery when he will have treatment. I'm just scared for the kids...for me," I admitted, looking into my mother's eyes with tears filling mine.

"You have to trust God that everything is going to be all right, and don't be afraid to let Him know how you're really feeling. It's okay to be afraid, but just know that God can give you the peace you need even in the midst of the storm. Okay, Sweetheart"

"Yes, Mom..." my voice muffled because my head was buried in her bosom.

We made it through dropping the bomb on my parents, but as Gary and I drove home, the dread that hung over us both knowing we had to break the news to our children held us hostage in a cocoon of silence. Thinking about each of my children, wondering how they would react and how our household would be from this week going forward was enough to make me want to ask Gary to run away from it all. *"Ha!"* I thought to myself, *"As if..."*

Chapter Five

GARY, JR.

"Gary, Baby, come back! Let us finish explaining this to you!" my mother called behind me.

Right, explain that your father has cancer, surgery, maybe radiation or chemo? I ain't talking about that with my parents today or any other day!

As soon as I slammed my bedroom door, I heard the door-bell ring. I opened it to listen so I could hear who was at the door.

"Hey, 'sup, Mikki. G's not available right now, but I'll tell him to call you," Gerald was explaining to my girl.

"Hold up, I got it," I said as I ran down the stairs.

"Bro, Mom and Dad still want to talk to us…"

"Whatever, Man, I'm out…tell them that," I told my brother as I grabbed Mikki's hand and walked out the door.

"What's wrong?" Mikki asked. "Can you slow down before you drag me down the street? Gary!"

"Just come on!"

"Where're we going? I thought we were going to watch a movie…"

"Forget all that!"

"Why?"

"Stop buggin', girl! If you're wanna roll, then let's go…if

not, I'mma just go 'head."

Mikki knew me well enough to know that when I got mad, I wasn't hearing nothing, so we didn't talk all the way to the playground down the street. When we got there, we sat on a bench, but I wouldn't look at her.

"G, can you tell me what's wrong? You're scaring me."

I sighed, and my whole body shuddered hard; I couldn't talk because I was not going to cry in front of my girl.

"Please tell me, Gary. Maybe I could help?"

Finally turning to look Michaela in the face, I told her, "If you can cure prostate cancer, then you can help me, otherwise…"

"You have prostate cancer?" she asked before I could finish talking.

"No! My father does…they're talking about operating on him and he might have radiation or chemotherapy. I mean, how does a man my father's age get cancer?"

"I'm so sorry," Mikki said, hugging me tight around my neck. "I'll be here for you, okay?"

I looked into Mikki's pretty brown eyes and the tears I tried to bury just came on their own. Holding me in her arms, my girl didn't say another word until I was ready to talk. *Man, this is some bull*! I kept thinking to myself over and over again.

"It's starting to get dark, Gary…are you ready to go home yet?"

"Can I come to your house? Not ready to go back to mine right now."

"You know you're always welcome. My Mom will be home from work soon, and I have to at least look like I'm doing homework," Mikki smiled.

"Aiight then."

The walk back to Mikki's was too fast. As much as I didn't want to go home, it still felt weird being able to see my house from down the street, but I made up my mind that I wasn't going back until much later tonight.

Around eleven that night, I got a text from Gerald saying my Dad wanted me home, so I thanked Michaela's Mom, Mrs. Chapman, for dinner and slowly walked home. I knew my parents were upset with me, but c'mon, they knew I was at Mikki's house, or one of my other friends. Running a few scenarios of how things were going to go down when I walked in the door, I was unprepared for the calm that I felt when I went into the house through the back door.

I was about to try to get upstairs to my room without anyone seeing me when I heard my father call me to join him in the den. Trying my best to act like I was okay, I sat in the chair across from the sofa where my father was sitting with only a lamp on next to him.

"Son, I know this is hard for you…it's hard for all of us. You know that we talk things out and we pray about them. Don't run out again on a family discussion upsetting your mother the way you did. Understood?"

"Aiight…"

"*Understood?*"

"Yes, Dad…understood."

"Let's give this another 24 hours and you and I can talk about this and what's going to happen moving forward. Anything you don't understand, I'll do my best to explain it to you. And Son? This is hard for me too, but I trust God to bring me through it. Got that?"

"Yes…"

"Let's head on up, and make sure you let your mother know you're back and you're okay. I want to get a good night's sleep," my Dad said with a half-smile on his face. I smiled too, because I know how Mom is when she's worried about one of us.

On my way to my room, I stopped by my parents' bedroom to kiss my mother and tell her I was okay knowing full well I was lying when I said it, but I never want her to worry about me because I can take care of myself. She's got enough to worry about with my Dad getting ready to go through this cancer stuff.

When I got to my room and shut the door, I took off my clothes, throwing each piece, wishing they were hard objects to hit someone with. Whoever it was I thought was to blame for my father being sick, I just wanted to beat them down, real talk. With that in mind, I headed for the shower knowing I wasn't going to sleep easy that night.

Chapter Six

TONYA

"Is he okay, Gary?"

"He says he is, but I know better than that...none of us is okay at this point," Gary answered, sitting down hard next to me on the bed.

"Did you talk to him about leaving the house without saying anything to us? He's so headstrong and..."

"I talked to him about it, Tonya. I just think we should just try to get some sleep tonight and put a little time between all of this and then talk about it again. I'll talk to Gary Jr. by himself in a day or so," Gary stressed. "How's Monét? I didn't get to check in on her yet."

"She was asleep about ten minutes ago when I looked in on her...it was a waste of time pulling the blanket back over her, it will be off before the morning."

Gary chuckled lightly as he headed towards our daughter's room to check on her, leaving me alone with my thoughts and fears. I have tried to hold up this strong front, but I can feel myself about to break down any second. Haven't been able to really put into words what to pray, so I'm sure God hears my heart; I just wish He would make things right again so our household can return to its normal routine.

It was determined that since the cancer had not spread, Gary would begin hormone therapy to stop his body from producing testosterone. It turns out that the cancer grows from it, so the best thing to do at this point is to stop it from producing altogether. My concern was the side effects and Gary's overall prognosis once the medicine was completed.

Lupron Depot™ was a suggested medication, but after Gary experienced swollen feet, decreased strength and increased sweating, Dr. Weiss put him on Trelstar™, which is a long-acting medicine that is administered by injection in the buttocks every two and a half months. Right now we don't know how long Gary will have to use the medication, however, he did have a slight urinary blockage that caused a problem briefly. Using a catheter was probably as painful for me as it was for him, but after a while everything seemed to go fine and Gary was able to return to work after his release from the doctor six weeks after his surgery.

Prayers from our families and congregation helped us to make it through the process, and our family was finally back to some sense of normalcy by the time school started back in September. My sons were now seniors on their way to college careers, and Monét was now in 7th grade, having gone from disliking boys to giggling about them with her friends. But there was always a prayer in my heart concerning my husband's recovery because there is no way I could stand for him to have to go through another cancer scare. I understood that the doctor said Gary was in remission, but I wanted God to give him complete healing.

Chapter Seven

GARY SR.

Having to come to terms with the fact that I had cancer took a lot out of me mentally and emotionally, but once the surgery was done and I was able to return to work, I trusted God that this was it. I'm told my prognosis looks good considering the survival rate for stage three prostate cancer is of a relative five years, still I'm believing that I will live to see my great grandchildren.

I'm not going to act like I was good through this whole process; there were times that I wanted to go and lay my head in my mother's lap the way I did when I was a kid, but now that I'm better her over-protective ways are grinding on my nerves. Like today, when she just happened to stop by and wouldn't let me sit and relax.

"Mom, I'm good…"

"You're my *only* son, you hear me? Where's Tonya anyway?" my mother inquired while she placed a pillow behind my head.

"Truth be told, I have no idea. I still don't need you to be treating me like a baby. Work was rough today and all I want to do is sit here and relax without a pillow behind my head. I'm no longer sick, Cecelia Simmons," I smiled.

"Mmmmmm hmmmmmmm, let me find out you're keeping

things from me like you did at first with this illness and I'm going to have you go get me a switch out the back yard," my mother joked, swatting me on my left thigh.

Flinching from the memory of the former thigh pain, I tried to act like I was about to get up but my mother's watchful eye didn't miss a thing. Before she could say a word, I told her it was just 'fake pain,' nothing was hurting me.

"Where is everybody? The boys don't come by and see me like that used to, and Monét has started hanging around the Hendersons…"

"Mom, have you looked at the guys lately? They're almost men and will be 18 on their next birthday. Monét's friends live by her grandparents' house, so she goes over there more often to be with them…"

"And where did you say your wife is today?" my mother's accusatory tone sounded in my ear, cutting me off.

"Don't recall saying where Tonya is, but maybe you know better than I do? Mom, don't start about Tonya today, hear? I thought all of that was behind you?"

"It is, it's just that you're shutting me out…I'm as much a part of this family as her parents are…"

"And the kids used to run to be at your house when they were younger, but they're growing up. The guys in particular, so let it go. It's not Tonya's fault and it certainly isn't mine. She's doing the best she can to keep up with them and take care of this household without you passing judgment on her every time you think something isn't going your way…"

"Gary! I know you're not talking to me this way!"

"Look, Mom, we've been through this, and quite honestly…I'm more than tired of it," I said, getting up to grab a snack from the kitchen. Still, it was strange for Tonya not to be home, but if she needed me, she would call.

On my heels, my mother starts sounding like I hurt her feelings, "It's just me in that big ole house, it's not like it was when you were growing up, or when the kids visited all the time. It gets lonely in there by myself."

"There it is, the truth. Why don't you ask Monét and her friends to have one of their sleepovers at your house?"

As soon as the suggestion crossed my lips, Tonya came in the door through the garage with her arms loaded with bags.

"I have them, Baby; why didn't you let me know you were here?" I asked, kissing my wife on her soft cheek. If my mother wasn't standing there watching, I would have lingered a while.

"Long day, and I know you've had a pretty long one yourself. Hi Cecelia," Tonya addressed my mother.

"Hey, Tonya...well, I'm going to get going, but tell Monét to call her Nana Cee so we can plan our sleepover date," my mother taunted in Tonya's direction as she left the kitchen headed for the front door.

"I'm not asking you what that is all about," Tonya shook her head in the negative. "There's a few more bags in my trunk. Close it when you're done."

The rest of the evening was the normal Simmons' household stuff with the guys barely making it in the house for curfew, and hearing Monét talking on the phone, giggling with her friends about whatever pre-teen girls talk about. I just sat back and listened in a way I can't ever remember doing, loving what I was hearing yet sensing that it was something that I will not get to enjoy for very long. I cannot explain what I felt in my spirit, but I never let on that it was bothering me.

Then there was this new 'urge' to make the men's ministry at church the best it could be and continue to mentor young boys. That's my calling, ministering to the pre-teen, teen and young adult men. Particularly to those whose fathers are absent for one reason or another, and it isn't easy. They come with so much anger that it seems we will never be able to break through, but being consistent with showing them love has knocked down many thick walls.

Lastly, I've felt for some time that I needed to put my affairs in order, making sure all three of my children's tuition savings were correct, as well as any trust money that would be issued a certain way once they entered college. Of course anything associated with the house would be taken care of as well so that Tonya would always be at ease concerning any household bills and repairs. Just some things that I probably should have taken care of long ago, but when you view life in your 20s and 30s, you never think about the possibility of leaving your family behind and them not being cared for properly.

Tonya knew about the funds set aside for our children, but she had no idea what I'd put together for her. There was no way I could possibly tell her how I had been feeling and the reasons I was doing all of this. It's a feeling, so why worry her unnecessarily?

"Hey, are you coming up?" Tonya suddenly appeared in front of me, interrupting my thoughts.

"I'll be up in a moment," I smiled.

"Are you okay?" she wanted to know, slightly tilting her head to the right.

"Of course, why?"

Kissing me sweetly on the lips, Tonya let me know she was going up and will be waiting for me. "I just know you're not going to stay too long…"

"Sounds like a dare to me," I told her jumping to my feet, chasing her up the stairs, allowing her a good head start before catching her as soon as we reached our bedroom door. Stopping to kiss my wife thoroughly, I heard Monét's door open.

"Eeeeeeeeeeewwwwwwww, I knew it. My parents, they are always kissing, yuck!" Monét said into the phone she was holding to her left ear.

"You better worry about getting off of that phone soon, young lady," Tonya said.

Ignoring her, Monét told her friend, "I'm about to hang up before I get in trouble with the 'love birds.' I know, right? I'm never going to do all that when I'm their age…"

The door closed on Monét's conversation, and Tonya and I couldn't help laughing at our daughter's innocence as we headed into our own bedroom to continue what we had started.

Chapter Seven

GARY JR.

"Yo, G., you better get in here before Mom and Dad notice you're not home," Gerald told me when I answered my phone.

"I'm coming, just open the window in the den and I'll come through there."

"Last time, Bruh, 'cause I don't want Mom going off on me when she gets at you."

"Yeah, yeah aiight, I'll be there in a few," I told my brother and hung up my phone.

"Fellas, fellas, gotta go…we'll get up tomorrow…" I told my boys, giving them each dap before I headed back towards home from the playground down the street. We're really not supposed to hang out there after dark, but that's the spot and it's where my boys and I ball.

As soon as I got to the house, I headed to the side of the house where the den is hoping Gerald opened the window wide enough for me to fit inside without making noise. I don't know why my parents don't just let us stay out as long as we want to since it won't be long before we're 18. Well, at least let me do it since Gerald is all about the books and whatever else it is he does. Girls are few and in between for him although they are always trying to get at him, he stays focused on his goals.

Sometimes I wish I was more like him...only sometimes.

"The doors in this house don't work?" my father asked as soon as my feet hit the floor.

"Uh ummm uh, Dad..."

"I'm listening."

Trying to think fast, I said, "I didn't want everybody to wake up hearing a door thinking somebody was breaking in."

"And you think I was born today, don't you? If you think I don't know about Gerald leaving a window up for you, you've got another *think* coming. Make this your last night coming in this house after curfew or through a window. Understood?"

"Yes, Dad..." I hated when my father made me feel like a 10 year-old. "Can we at least get another hour..."

"We're not negotiating anything tonight. Until such time, if your mother ever gets upset behind your behavior in this house, you and I are going to have a talk without words. Are we clear?"

"Yes..."

I watched my father head upstairs as I went to the kitchen to find a snack and a drink. My parents think everything is good now that my Dad is better and back to work, but that cancer stuff messed my head up. I never thought that people that serve God get sick like that, but I guess that's not realistic. We've been taught to believe God all of our lives, so this should be a no-brainer for me, but it's not. Why my father and why did he have to go through all of that stuff to get better. Isn't God supposed to heal people immediately? What about the stories in the Bible when Jesus healed people, even brought them back from the dead? Don't we have those benefits too?

These thoughts mess with my head almost every day unless I keep myself really busy with my boys or Mikki. Otherwise, quiet time means my mind won't stop, and me not wanting to be at home is my way of dealing with it. Speaking of Mikki, I probably would have never thought about these things if she didn't ask me those questions. I told her what my parents said, but I just couldn't help thinking there was good reason to find answers to those same questions that are now posted up in my head like permanent ink.

Downing a bottle of water, I grab a pack of cookies off of the counter and head upstairs to my room. Before I could walk past Gerald's room, he calls my name. Sticking my head in his bedroom door, I wait to hear what he has to say.

"Dad caught you, huh?"

"Yeah, but it's cool…"

Gerald smirked at me and kept typing away on his laptop, his way of dismissing me. I continued to my room trying to figure out what I was going to get into until I was ready to go to sleep. One thing was sure…it wasn't coming easy.

Chapter Seven

TONYA

"What do you mean Brian's cheating? Are you sure, Lisa?"

"How sure can I be when I stopped by his office after hours and walked in on him and his new little medical student he's mentoring," Lisa told me with distress in her voice.

"You're saying he was mentoring her after the office closed?

"Oh, he was mentoring her all right...with her tail bent over the front of his desk while he was banging her from behind telling her to say his name!" Lisa screamed.

"Oh my Lord, Lisa, why didn't you just tell me that? What are you going to do, what did he do, I mean...wow!"

"What else? Jumped up trying to get their clothes up, but not before I punched Brian in his face and grabbed that stank thang by her nasty weave and wrapped it around her neck and choked her to tears!" Lisa screamed, unable to contain her temper.

At first I was silent, praying while Lisa sniffled and broke into a soft sob on the other end of the phone. Still unsure as to what to say, my heart clenched with pain as I listened to my best friend's heartbroken cry.

"Leese, I know you may not know what you want to do,

but I'm here for you. Let me know if there is anything I can do to help…ok?"

"Thanks, Tonya…I already know what I'm going to do. I'll be there by the end of August so I will have time to straighten up some things here and come home. My mother is finally going to get her wish," Lisa told me, breaking down in tears again.

"You've decided to move back home? Are you sure you can't work it out with Brian?"

"Are you out of your mind? He crossed a line that he cannot fix…me being suspicious and not finding anything is one thing, but to see my husband up in some tramp ain't forgivable in this lifetime or the next. I'm done! No marriage counseling, prayer or temporary separation is going to fix this mess," Lisa emphatically stated, although her voice quivered.

"Are you trying to tell me this isn't the first time? Because it sounds to me that you've been going through some things for a while now," I stated with suspicion of my own.

After a few minutes of silence, Lisa began to tell me how things changed after the birth of her son and the weight she couldn't seem to lose. Since there were no major problems with their marriage, she and Brian continued to live life as usual until her husband and his partner decided to mentor medical students a few years ago. Lisa supported their decision and would help the office staff from time-to-time to ensure that records were accurate so the students could always reach back for proof of their time in the office.

"So much for having my husband's back…he had his hands on a few of the student's 'back,' of this I'm sure. I don't care how many years we've been together, this is way past crossing the line. So you know what I'm doing? I'll tell you! I'm slowly but surely shipping things I want to New Jersey to my parents' house so that when me and the kids come for vacation in a few weeks, we'll actually be staying," Lisa revealed.

"If that's your decision, I'll be the last one to try and talk you out of it, Lisa."

"Thanks, Tonya, I really appreciate that. At least that way, if I feel like I've made a mistake, I only have myself to blame."

"You've got *that* right," I laughed, trying to break up the mood.

Laughing, Lisa asked me, "How's Gary doing? I'm dropping all of my sob-sad life messes on you and didn't even think
to ask."

"He's good, and he's still cancer-free. God is good, you
know?"

"I'm glad to hear that…heard from that crazy Denise?"

"A few weeks back, talking about she thinks she's going
through menopause. I think she needs to see her gynecologist
and find out why she's missed her last couple of monthly visitors. We're not that old, are we?" I chuckled.

"I ain't claiming nothing, especially after I wash these few
gray soldiers out of my head, humph! I've lost a good 60 pounds
and I will be buying myself a brand new wardrobe, hairdo and a
day at the spa on Mr. Brian before you all see me in Jersey. It's
time for the new me, Honey, and I'm going to be working it too,
you hear me?" Lisa declared.

We laughed and talked some more, Lisa promising to let
me know her traveling plans while I made my way to the kitch-
en to figure out dinner for the evening. Today was the first day I
really had a break all summer and cooking really was not on the
top of my list, but I promised my husband I would fix something
light.

Once I finished fixing a large grilled chicken salad and
some homemade rolls, my crew started making their way home.
Most nights we are not able to sit at the table for a family dinner,
so I've reluctantly started getting used to the staggered sched-
ule, with the exception of Monét. She is usually the only one
coming into the kitchen by our set dinner hour with Gary right
behind her, if he's not held at work for one reason or another.

Dinner was uneventful with normal family talk as we
discussed the upcoming school year and expectations of our
children. Of course Gary Jr. was the last one to join us, but
he wasn't too interested in talking about school with his mind
constantly on football and hell week that was scheduled to take
place the week before school started. His excitement was infec-
tious and we soon found ourselves laughing and sharing how we
would split our time between the NBA for Gerald and the NFL

for Gary Jr.

"I'm telling you, I'm planning to go all the way straight to the NFL, then maybe I'll marry Mikki and have a few kiddies and..."

"Whoa, son, let's get through the 12ᵗʰ grade first," Gary laughed. "Didn't know you were that serious about Mikki?"

"Why do you think he can hardly get in the house on time at night?" Gerald teased, taking a punch from his brother.

"All I know is, the kids better not come before the college education or the marriage license or there will be problems," I interjected as I began clearing the dishes. "Monét , I want you to get on these dishes before the phone calls and the TV."

"Get to it, you little pest," Gary Jr. teased, mushing Monét 's head.

"Stop! Dad, did you see what Gary did?"

"Keep your hands off of your little sister; you're supposed to protect her, not harm her," Gary said, giving his daughter a hug. Monét leaned her head to the side and stuck her tongue out at her brother.

"Brat!"

"Ha ha, that's what you get," Monét teased her brother.

"Ever since she started wearing those sling shots, the little brat thinks she's growing up," Gary Jr. continued to tease his sister.

"Ooooooooooh, Mom, did you hear him? I am a pre-teen now, thank you very much," Monét stated emphatically. "Just because I don't have big balloons like Mikki..."

"All right, that's enough!"

"You heard your mother," Gary told our children as he walked out of the kitchen. Still my children teased each other until I told Monét to help me clean the kitchen.

The familiar sounds of our household was so comforting to me as we went about our lives, something I missed tremendously when Gary was going through treatment and dealing with cancer. Cherishing the moment and the memories have become so important to me, especially with our sons embarking on manhood and the rest of their lives. Thankfully Gary will be here to help them make that transition while I look forward to the opportunity to help our daughter through her teen years. We agreed to grow older together, Gary and I, and it's a little bitter-sweet to watch our children heading towards adulthood.

Chapter Eight

GARY JR.

Man, I was so glad when school started again. Not for the school work, but for the football team; doing my work was only part of the deal to keep me on the team. Making sure I had a "B" or "C" average was part of my agreement with my parents to remain there. My biggest challenge so far this semester wasn't doing my work, or putting it in on the field; it was Mikki. One minute she was with me, and the next minute she was trying to bail.

"You coming over or not?"

"It's not that I don't want to, G, but you're not listening to me...I'm not ready..."

"Do you know how long you've been telling me this? Why not? We've been together since we were kids, and now..."

"And now you think you're an adult. I don't!" Mikki fumed with her arms crossed over her big breasts.

I turned Mikki's frowned up face back to me and kissed her lips, rubbed her arms so I could touch one of her boobs by "accident," and said, "Babe...this thing we got right here? It's not going anywhere...ok? You believe me?"

"Gary, I'm scared...plus my Mom will not be happy with me."

"I thought she told you to let her know when you need birth

control."

"She did, but it's only because one of my cousins had a baby at 16, not because we ever really talked about sex. My mother just wants to make sure I don't embarrass her in front of our family and friends. I don't want to do it..."

"Okay then, I'll wait on you. You're my girl, and I love you...I can wait," I told her, pulling Mikki to me to kiss her full lips. "Still want to come over?"

"Yes..."

Mikki always waited for me to finish football practice and attended all of our home games to show her support and to make sure the girls knew that I was spoken for. I've never cheated, but I'll be lying if I didn't think about doing it since my hormones have been going crazy for my girl and she didn't want to help me keep them under control.

When we arrived at my house, no one was at home, so I convinced Mikki to go with me to the basement to watch TV in my father's office and man cave. Before long, we were kissing, rubbing and touching and I found my way around the snaps on the front of Mikki's bra. Maaaaaan, those things popped out and sprung up so quickly, I almost lost my grip on her lips. Hearing her moans almost sent me crazy! Just as I was about to pull Mikki's shirt above her head, I heard my father's voice say, "Son?"

Jumping up and pulling her shirt down, Mikki started looking for her jacket, and I stood up to block her from my father's view.

"No need to ask what's going on down here, do I?"

"Dad..."

"Mikki, I'll give you a few minutes to get yourself together. Gary, you walk her home and come right back...we need to talk."

"Dad, it's not..."

"We'll talk when you get back here," my father said as he went back up the basement steps.

By this time Michaela had started crying and I felt so bad. When I reached out to touch her, she pulled away from me, putting her book bag on her shoulder.

"Mikki, I'm so sorry..."

"No! Too late for sorry...now your father probably thinks I'm some kind of whore or something, and he's going to tell your Mom. You know what? Don't walk me home, I know my way," Mikki said, pushing past me to go up the stairs.

"Michaela, I'm walking you home," I told her when I caught up with her. "I'm in enough trouble with my father, so I'm doing what he told me to do."

It was hard to walk Mikki home with her speed walking down the street. No matter how many times I called her name, she just held up her hand signaling for me to be quiet. Before she made it to her driveway, I ran up to her and grabbed her in a bear hug, not letting her move.

"Gary, turn me loose! I am so mad at you right now! Stoooooooooppppppp!"

"Just listen to me, will you please? Stop trying to get away from me because you know you can't. Now listen...I'm going to tell my father the truth about this, okay? I'll let him know that it was all me and we kind of got caught up...he's a man, he understands. Trust me on this, he won't think bad things about you. That's my word."

Instead of answering me, Mikki just stared into my eyes like she was going to kill me as soon as I let her go. I had no plans of releasing her until she calmed down because I wasn't going to let her hit me.

Sighing heavily and shuddering with the cry she was trying to hold in, Mikki agreed and I let her go. We stood there looking at each other for a few minutes, and then my eyes wandered from her face down her body to her feet and back to her face. My girl is beautiful! Mikki has these big pretty eyes that change from dark brown to light brown depending on her mood that just soaks me in when she looks at me. I was hooked when we became friends over ten years ago and we were little kids. Back then she was a tall string bean, but now? Now my baby is hot! Mikki went from flat to having 36DD joints, a skinny waist, bootie for days and hips that make me want to slap on them all the time. Her small feet don't seem to go with her size 8, 5'8" body, but when I look at her pretty face and light cocoa skin, I have to admit that I melt like a sucker.

Once more, I pulled Michaela into my arms, gently this time, and held her. I really love this girl, and I promised her that I would do my best to curb my growing appetite to get closer to her.

"Promise me you will tell your Dad this was all about you…and let your parents know that I'm going to come and apologize tomorrow after school. I still feel bad, Gary."

"I know…I'll tell them. Go on inside, Babe. I've got to go home and get snapped on by my Pops."

"Is he going to yell?"

"I can tell you right now, we're only going to see each other in school for about a week," I laughed, but I wasn't too happy about that.

"He's actually going to put you on punishment?" Mikki wanted to know.

"No telling with my Dad, so I'll text you later," I said, kissing Mikki once more before I headed back down the street to my house.

The short walk home was spent trying to figure out how I was going to tell my father I almost pressured Mikki into having sex with me. I can see his disappointed face and hear what he was going to say before he said it. My father has been drilling into me and Gerald since we were little kids about respecting girls and women, and then adding that we should never force a girl to have sex, even if we convince them they want it as much as we do. What am I supposed to do when the girls be trying to put it in my hand? I've been ignoring it, but it's getting harder when I have a girl and I can't do nothing. If Mikki would let me do something, or she do something to me, maybe I can take my mind and the edge off of my urges.

I knew that everybody was home when I walked in the door, but my father refused to wait until after dinner to address the issue. He told me to meet him in the same place I was about to get it in with Michaela. That's not even cool.

"Have a seat…"

"Before you say anything, Dad, can I please explain about today?"

"You know what? That might be a good idea. Why don't you tell me what went on down here. For right now, I'm going to try not to believe what I know I saw. Go on."

"See first, I want you to know that Mikki wasn't really the one doing anything, and she's sorry…and so am I," I began to explain.

My father acknowledged what I said with a nod and urged me to continue. Before I knew anything, I just came clean with him, telling him that I haven't had sex. Mikki is my girl and I respect her and all, but it's really getting hard for me not to want more from her.

"So tell me something, Son…what 'more' are you giving Michaela?"

"What do you mean?"

"You're telling me you want more from Mikki, but what is the 'more' you're going to be giving her? Marriage or the promise of it? You will be taking her most precious gift and the best you can do is to continue being her boyfriend, if sleeping together doesn't change the dynamics."

I sat there for a moment with what I know must have looked like the "dumb look" on my face because I really did not understand what my father was trying to tell me, and then he broke it down for me.

"If you don't forget anything I tell you tonight, I want you to remember that you are accountable to God first for your actions concerning any young lady. You are not married to Mikki, and according to what you've shared, neither of you has decided to have sex…yet. When you do, it is not just a physical act, but your spirit and your soul is involved. It's a spiritual coming together that ties your souls together that only God can break… either she will find herself wanting you and you not wanting her, or vice versa…or both of you wanting each other and not being able to decide what to do with your relationship. Sex is for marriage, period. If you're not mature enough to handle what comes with having sex, then you need to leave it alone.

"Dad, how do you know this? You and Mom waited until you got married…I don't know how you waited," I stressed.

"For one, my mother always taught me that I shouldn't just

be concerned about the young lady, but for myself. She told me that I didn't want to start sharing all the girls I'd had sex with, with the woman I will want to marry one day. That hit me deep when she explained the possibility of STDs being spread from one person to another…and now that I know better according to God's Word, it also applies spiritually. All that baggage you carry from one relationship to another is too much. When I met your Mom, she wasn't having it…and I fell in love with her almost from the start; but ultimately, I've respected her and wouldn't dare do anything to hurt her.

"You owe Mikki an apology if you haven't already done so…this flesh is going to act like flesh, Gary. Rub on it, kiss on it, caress it…well, it's going to start reacting the way it's supposed to, and if you keep at it long enough, a fire you can't put out is going to ignite. Then you have to deal with the consequences of your actions after the fact…a baby, an STD, a stalker…"

"Stalker? Are you for real, Dad?"

"You don't want to find that out, Son. Men and women are wired differently; while some men can come and do their deed and go without any emotional ties, women sometimes equate sex with love and commitment without the words being said. Like I told you, that is a woman's most precious gift, and when she gives it away, she's going to want that 'more' you mentioned, and it won't consist of just being your bed buddy. She's going to want all of you forever. And one more thing…don't awaken love before its time when you have no intentions of being honorable."

I had a lot to think about, that's for sure. Not that I don't believe what my father was saying, but man, I still don't know what I'm going to do. The best part about talking with my Dad is that he didn't blast me or put me on punishment. Too old anyway. He even told me to tell Mikki that no apology was necessary because he wasn't going to tell my Mom what happened unless it happens again. Talk about dodging a bullet? My Pops is cool for real…besides, I wouldn't be able to take the hurt look my mother would wear on her face every time she would look at me if he did tell her.

Chapter Eight

GARY SR.

"Tonya, we're running late, Baby."

"I'm coming! I just got off the phone with my mother to make sure your daughter found her way over there after she left Dana's house. We'll get good seats, no worries. Where is Gary Jr.?"

"He left with Mike and Michaela headed to the school. Maybe we should have asked them to save us some seats..."

"What?"

"Nothing...are you ready?" I asked my wife.

The look Tonya gave me was my warning to stop bugging her, but I was so excited to get to the school gym to watch Gerald play. He was a starting point guard, standing at 6'2" and weighing in at about 180 pounds. I could see the potential of him making it all the way to the NBA with the skills he already possessed on the court. Having an analytical and strategic mind helped him with calling plays on the court; that along with his skills could definitely take him all the way. To say that I was more than pleased...well, it was an understatement.

Once I helped my wife with her coat, we headed for the car and was soon on our way to Stoney Brook High School. Our old alma mater was holding up really well, and it still looked pretty much the same with maybe a few new changes. Not only was I proud to have attended high school here, I was honored that my sons were leaving an indelible mark behind so that possibly their children will get to see that they added to the school and not taken anything away but a good education.

As soon as we found our seats, the buzzer sounded signaling the beginning of the game and my eyes were immediately glued to the court with my focus on Gerald. Mind you, his own personal cheering section was seated directly behind Tonya and me, getting on my wife's last nerve. Every time Gerald made a good play or his name was called over the loud speaker, the girls would do a special cheer with Gerald's number. It wasn't until half time that we were able to hear their conversation.

"I'm telling you, I'mma get with that *fiiiiiiiiiiiine* piece of chocolate," one girl stated.

"Oh honey *please*, Gerald Simmons ain't hardly checkin' for you...you see these 'make a baby' hips I got? We gonna make us some pretty babies one day," another girl commented.

"Nuh uh, we already kickin' it, it's just a matter of time before I get him to smash and ain't none a y'all..." the third young lady chimed in before Tonya turned around.

"Contrary to popular belief, neither one of you will get with Gerald Simmons," Tonya glared at the girls causing their conversation to cease immediately.

"Not for nothing, but uh, don't you think you too old to be feelin' a young dude like that? I mean, I know you might get down with that cougar stuff and all, but *dang!*" the first young lady commented and joined in with her friends laughing at my wife's expense. That's when I turned around.

"No, I'm a *lioness*, and you'd *better* watch your mouth," Tonya admonished the girl as calmly as she could.

"Oooooooh, so she *said that!*" one of the other girls yelled out, clapping her hands with each word.

That was it, I had to say something before my wife forgot she was saved and allowed her maternal instincts to cause her to go to jail.

"Ladies, you will respect my wife, the mother of my son that you are so openly talking about. Yes, we're Gerald Simmons' parents."

It was quiet for close to three minutes, but I could still hear them when they started whispering behind us. One of them said there was no way they could have known who Gerald's parents were, but he definitely took after his father, looks and all.

"Girl, I wonder how many fine men are in their family," one of the girls whispered to the other. The conversation swiftly changed to other things while we prepared to watch the second half of the game.

The game ended with a score of 66 to 60, the Stoney Brook Clippers winning and clinching the playoffs! I was just as excited as the players and I couldn't wait for my son to emerge from the locker room so I could let him know. Actually, I didn't think the team would make it into the locker room once the final buzzer rang and the fans emerged upon them on the court. Gerald had 12 points and 15 assists which, no doubt, helped his team to win. He never took credit for his hard work for the team, so when they made him the team captain, I was not surprised. Now on to the playoffs! My chest and my head was swollen with pride for my son and the team.

There was a lot of fanfare, the local newspaper taking pictures and fans clamoring around to get a chance to take pictures with the players. Gerald called his mother and me over so that we could all take pictures together. Gary Jr. made sure he was jumping up in the background before he took out his cell phone to take pictures of his mother, Gerald and I in different frames. I cannot remember feeling so proud of both of my sons…Gary Jr.'s team clinched the state football championship and, in spite of his average grades, colleges were looking at him. Gerald has been scouted since his junior year, so the boys are still in the midst of trying to decide which school to choose. It's a harder choice for Gerald due to the several choices he has, while Gary Jr. has already decided he would attend a historically black college or university, something neither Tonya nor I did.

Once everything calmed down and we were able to head for the car, our sons informed us that they were headed out to celebrate with the team and the girls that had been sitting behind

Tonya and I in the stands walked up to Gerald to talk to him.

"Heeeeeeeeeey, Gerald, where y'all headed?" one of the girls asked.

"We're going to that pizza spot on Second. Y'all coming?" Gerald responded to the girl.

"Excuse me a second...Gerald, can I talk to you before you go?" Tonya interrupted.

Stepping in, I told Tonya to talk to him when he came in, not in front of his peers. She was none too happy about that, but my wife has to remember that our sons are quickly becoming young men and we have to back off at times. Especially be mindful to choose our battles wisely or behind closed doors. At least Tonya waited until we were in the car on the way home before she let me know how she felt about my actions.

"Gary, I was just going to ask him if he knew that girl. I know I don't need to tell you that I don't like her with her fast tail self," Tonya stated with her arms folded.

"Sweety, it's not that serious, believe me. Gerald is not even dating a particular girl, so don't worry. He has a good head on his shoulders..."

"Until one of those little hot tails talk him into finding out what he's missing! One mistake can mess up his scholarships, and *I'm* going to do everything I can to make sure no babies come here without a college degree and a marriage certificate," Tonya declared.

"Babe, we're talking about teens here, and they will be considered grown according to the law..."

"I don't care what the law says! They are *still my sons*, Gary!" Tonya's voice broke.

I knew the tears were close behind, so I decided to wait until we made it home to talk about it again. My wife is having trouble letting our sons go, but she has no choice. Once they make up their minds where they want to go to school, there may be no way for us to get to them like we can now. For that matter, they very well may choose to attend college out of state. If they do, there will be plenty of sleepless nights for me.

Chapter Nine

TONYA

College tours, football, basketball, school dances, prom, year books, class rings...it was so overwhelming since we had to do it double, but I would not have it any other way. Yes, my sons are young men and I have to accept it, but I certainly do not have to like it. I find myself looking at their baby pictures almost every day wondering just where in the world all of the time went. Gary Jr. and Gerald may be fraternal twins, but if it were not for the fact that Gerald is an inch taller and Gary Jr. is a little heavier than Gerald, it would be harder to tell them apart for most people. Trust me, I learned who was who by their second day on this earth just by looking at them, and their personalities are exact opposites.

I tell you what, God must have heard my prayer because both of my sons decided to attend the University at Lincoln in Pennsylvania. Gerald has practically a free ride with the scholarships he earned and Gary Jr.'s tuition will have to be paid by his parents with a little help from grants and a small scholarship for football. Either way, we are blessed with some good guys and I knew before they left for college it was going to be harder on me than it was on them.

Gary and I decided once we accompanied are sons to the

college campus that will be educating them for the next four years, a vacation is going to happen for just the two of us. The nest is almost empty and I don't even want to think about Monét going off to college any time soon.

The campus was a madhouse with students and parents trying to check in, pick up dorm room keys and begin unpacking. The guys, thankfully, ended up in the same dorm that housed the athletes. The unfortunate thing was, they were on different floors and on opposite ends of the building. Gary went with Gerald to help him and I went with Gary Jr. to get him settled in. I'm sure neither of the boys wanted my help, but it had to be one or the other. Only they didn't know that I would be involved with both of their living quarters. I had to know what the rooms looked like, how clean they were and clean them anyway, put their clothing away and make sure the beds were cleaned and sprayed down. Afterwards the TV and games came out and the guys made themselves at home. However, we agreed to go have dinner together before Gary and I headed back to New Jersey.

Halfway through dinner is when my husband decided to let his sons know what he expected out of them concerning their grades and athleticism.

"You're embarking on the rest of your adult lives and you know how you've been raised. I don't want to hear anything contrary to your upbringing…that includes drinking, drugs, sex or anything you will find yourself in trouble for. Understood?"

"We're clear, Pops," Gary Jr. assured his father.

"Do you remember when you told me that you're both old enough to protect your Mom? I want you to always keep that in your mind. If you don't do well here, you won't have a leg to stand on when it comes to your mother. You need more than brawn to protect her, you need brains as well. Every battle isn't physical, so school will help to prepare you for the many battles that will come your way in this life. Got me?"

"Wait, Dad, what do you mean we can protect Mom? You said that you're here to protect her," Gerald said, his brow creased.

"Son, I am here to protect her, but now that you're grown men, you can do it as well…you know, in addition to what I do.

Not instead of me."

"Oh cool, we thought you were trying to tell us something," Gary Jr. stated, relief easing the tension that had built up in his shoulders.

"No one asked me what advice I have for you," I added. "When my three men get together, they act like I'm not in the room."

"Aw, Mom, we already know what you're going to say. Dad's talks are short; yours can go on for a while," Gary Jr. joked, ducking to miss the hit he knew I was going to throw.

"Ok smarty, tell me something…what's going on with you and Michaela?"

"We're good…she's going to Temple and we plan to stay together. When you and Dad let me and Gerald get cars, I can visit her on campus…"

"That's why I'm so happy the school does not allow freshmen to have cars on campus. None of that visiting each other's dorms…"

"And she wonders why we don't say anything to her?" Gary Jr. told Gerald.

Once the laughter died down, I told my son that I was curious about his relationship with Michaela because his Dad and I have been together since our senior year of high school.

"G and Mikki been kicking it since pop cycles and hop scotch, so they might as well go on and get married right out of college," Gerald commented with a smirk.

"Pretty much, but I like our relationship the way it is. No rush, Mom, trust me on that."

"I hope it doesn't mean you're planning to be with other girls now that there are so many to choose from at this college," I stated rather than asked.

"Mikki's my girl, we're good."

The ride home was quiet and reflective, me with my thoughts and Gary with his. I am still trying to wrap my mind around the fact that we just took our two sons to college at the same time. Not one this year and another in the next year or so, but both of them. The house is going to be so quiet, and now with Monét wrapped up into her friends and other activities, she only needs me to drop her off at the mall instead of shopping with her unless it's for school clothes. I realized I do not have babies any more, but I didn't know it would hurt so badly.

"Hey, Baby, you want to see if we can get a suite for the rest of the week? I don't know if I even want to go back home."

"I thought you had some things you wanted to do tomorrow? I was planning to head into the office for at least half the day," Gary told me while looking from me to the road.

"Do you have to go in? We haven't done anything at the spur of the moment in a long time. I'm sure my Mom won't mind keeping Monét until Sunday after church..."

"So that means we have to go pack a bag...I'll think about it and let you know by the time we get to the house. I'm tired."

"Please, I need this. Gary? I promise to let you rest until tomorrow morning, but I don't want you to go to work...just hang out together like we did when we didn't have kids. We might as well get a practice run because you know it won't be long before everybody is gone."

"Let's not worry about that until the time comes," Gary said around a yawn. "Do you feel like driving so I can catch a quick nap?"

"Stop at the Dunkin Donuts coming up so I can grab a cup of tea and then I'll drive. You do look tired."

Truth be told, my husband has been telling me he's tired a lot lately; getting a bit concerned about that. As always Gary tells me he's fine, he's been working hard and not taking any real time for himself. That much may be true, but I will pack us both a bag and drive to a nice hotel after we get home because he's going to get some rest.

After a wonderful weekend with my husband, the light was blinking on the top of left corner of our house phones when we came home from church. I started to ignore it, but didn't want to miss any important messages. The lone message asked Gary to call Dr. Weiss's office at his earliest convenience. I didn't remember Gary going to see the doctor, but he has to go every two and a half months to monitor his progress. Waiting until we sat down to dinner to tell him, I wasn't expecting my husband to try to blow me off about it.

"No worries, Tonya, I'll call him back some time tomorrow."

"When did you go see him?" I wanted to know.

"A little over a week or so ago. I didn't need you to go. It's handled," Gary told me, getting up from the table after only half eaten his dinner.

"Daddy, you're not hungry?" Monét asked her father.

"Not really, Baby Girl…Tonya, I'm going to lay down. Do you mind waking me around 7 so we won't be late for church tonight?"

I simply nodded because had I opened my mouth, I would have torn into him like his life depended on it because I *know* there is something going on. He's starting to get tired a lot like before and so help me God if he's keeping anything from me, we're going to blows. My feelings must have been showing all over my face because Monét asked to be excused from the table as soon as she finished eating.

After I cleaned the kitchen, I went upstairs to the bedroom to find my husband simply resting, not sleeping. I climbed on the bed with Gary and wrapped one of my arms around his waist and snuggled up close and listened to the silence for a while, enjoying the peace of just being still. When Gary took a deep breath and let it out slowly, it was time for us to talk.

"Out with it!"

"What?"

"Why won't you tell me? We're not going around the bush on this, I want to know what's going on with you right now! You've been getting tired again, and you're either sleeping or laying around. Let's go, put it out there so we can deal with it together," I told Gary.

"Tonya, come on and lay back down. It's nothing," Gary said, pushing the pillow up under his head.

"Are you serious? Tell me you're not because we need to…"

Before I could finish my sentence, Gary grabs me, wrestles me down on the bed and held me there with his body. I tried to get up, any effort thwarted by my husband's sweet kisses that flooded my face. I decided to give in and let Gary have his way. Our intimate moments don't come as often as they once did before he got sick, so we took full advantage of our time.

A few hours later I was awakened by a knock on the bedroom door.

"Mom! Dad! It's seven!" Monét's voice penetrated the door.

"Okay…we're up," came my sleep-filled response.

"I thought *old people* take naps…" I heard Monét say as she walked away from the door.

I looked over at Gary, he looked at me and we couldn't help but to laugh. I told him Monét was *his* daughter, but that mouth came from Cecelia Simmons.

Chapter Ten

GARY SR.

Tonya made sure to remind me to call Dr. Weiss back and tried her best to get information out of me that I just didn't have...or wouldn't give. I knew the verdict before I ever called the doctor back. My numbers don't look so good all of a sudden, and he wanted me in his office for further testing and evaluation. It was going to have to wait because I had a trip planned for me and my wife and nothing was going to dampen my spirits and keep me from enjoying our time together.

"Baby, come on, they're calling our seats," Tonya said, grabbing me by my shirt sleeve, pulling me along with her.

"Slow down, they're not going to leave us," I chuckled. My wife is more than excited about this trip.

Tonya and I have not really gone anywhere alone in all the years we've been married unless it included the kids in some way, so I owed her a vacation and I wanted to do something that would not keep us away from home for too long. I booked a five-days, four-night cruise to the Bahamas with Royale Caribbean on the Majestic Sea Merchant. Our stops are Nassau, Bahamas, CocoCay Beach, Key West Florida and back to Miami, Florida. My wife only knows that we are going on a cruise; I refused to give her any details until we board the ship so that she can see everything for herself.

It wasn't long before the airplane was in the air and we were relaxed in our seats waiting on a light snack to be served. I was tired already and planned to take a nap if I could keep my wife from leaning over my lap to look out of the window.

"Sweety, why don't we switch seats?"

"You know I don't like sitting next to the window, Gary. It's beautiful to look at though," Tonya told me, kissing me on my cheek before she settled back in her seat.

We talked about everything from the kids to retirement and back before I found myself waking up to Tonya nudging me awake. Strange…I didn't feel myself fall asleep.

"We've landed, wake up, sleepyhead," Tonya said as she unbuckled her seatbelt.

"You buckled me in?" I asked around a stretch and a yawn.

"Who else? Let's get cracking so we can start this vacation proper, Baby!"

"I'll grab the stuff up there…" I told my wife as I pulled myself up from the seat.

I had to get myself together and act like I wasn't as tired as I was all for Tonya, but it was far from easy. The walk to baggage claim and out to the area to catch the shuttle to the ship was no picnic. Being able to finally get out in the air helped a lot, but as soon as we walked out of the doors of the airport, Tonya was overcome quickly by the heat.

"Oh my, Lord! Are you kidding me? This ain't hot, it's *haught*!" Tonya declared, pulling her short sleeve shirt over her head. "I can't believe it's this hot!"

"What did you expect for the end of August? And you'd better thank God you have a tank on under that shirt or you and I would have big problems out here," I warned my wife.

"As if I would be out here in public stripping, Gary."

"You just whipped that shirt off like you were in your bedroom or something; I'm sure I'm not the only who thought you were about to get naked out here," I laughed.

"Hot as it is, naked just might be the only way to go. Can we please find that shuttle so we can get in some air conditioning? Whew! This heat is unreal."

Finding the shuttle was easy, and waiting on it allowed me some time to catch my breath and regroup so I could pull myself together. I did not want to tell my wife what I already knew was going on with me without hearing the doctor's report. I ache in a way I never have in my life…it feels like it's in my bones or close to it. Actually, I wish they would have removed everything…at least then I may have had a chance for a full recovery without reoccurrence.

"Baby? I think our shuttle is coming in," Tonya told me, interrupting my thoughts.

Gathering our suitcases, we followed the other people who were also waiting to take the shuttle to the cruise line. We were able to board pretty quickly, and Tonya enjoyed looking out of the window as we passed through Miami.

"You know I'm trying to see if we pass through any neighborhoods we see on First 48, right?" Tonya stated, never turning to look at me. "We used to see how beautiful Miami was before that show…it's still nice here, just too hot!

I chuckled at my wife's observation, but once we made it to the ship and turned our luggage over to them, finding a nice place to sit on the deck was a welcome treat. The breeze off of the ocean was just what I needed, and the view of Star Island intrigued my wife. She started naming celebrities that have residences there and how exclusive it looked from where we were sitting.

"Do you think our next vacation can be to Star Island? I've heard about the nice hotels and the sights there…it could be really romantic," Tonya told me, holding on to my hand.

"Oh no, I'm not going there."

"Why? It's beautiful! You can see that from here."

"Maybe you should go with Lisa and Denise so you can shop and do all of that walking. I'm not up for that, Baby."

"You know what? That might be a good idea. I'm going to take a picture right now and send it to my girls and maybe we can take a trip next summer….ooooooh they are going to be too excited! Especially Lisa since she's made up her mind that she is done with Brian. They were never able to work things out before she made it here last week," Tonya expressed.

"I'm sorry to hear that, really. Brian's an all right guy…"

"Until he started cheating on Lisa and get this, Baby, he didn't stop," Tonya interrupted me to say. "He finally broke down and told Lisa that he feels they have gone as far as they could together."

"Say what? What does that supposed to mean?" I wanted to know.

"Heck if I know. Lisa said her in-laws are angry with their son, but they couldn't convince him to stay and work things out with Lisa. He's going to regret it, that's for sure."

"What is Denise up to these days?" I asked to change the subject.

"Crazy as ever. Dating the bass player in her church who is about 10 years or so younger than she is. The last time I spoke to her, Denise decided to forego the meds her doctor put her on to help regulate her because she's premenopausal. I told her that was a bad move, but she insisted the side effects was worse than the problems she was already having," my wife explained to me.

"I'm glad I'm a man, so let's leave that right there," I laughed.

By the time we pulled out into the ocean, I felt my eyes drift shut to the shouts of bon voyage and only opened them when my wife insisted that perhaps we head to our cabin to get some rest before our dinner hour. I was thankful Tonya did not want to walk around the ship because I was past exhausted. Falling back to sleep once we entered our cabin was easy, but waking up for dinner was a bit too much. However, I wanted to please my wife on this trip, so I prayed for strength to do just that… and I prayed the next four nights would be one of the best times I've ever shared with my wife. Praying it would not be our last.

Chapter Eleven

TONYA

We did it all on our cruise, from shopping to eating, to lounging on the deck, enjoying the pool late at night while most people were doing other things, and spending intimate moments alone in our beautiful cabin suite. The view was marvelous! CocoCay beach had the whitest powdery soft sand I'd ever seen in my life, and the ocean was blue and magnificent. We could see the fish and other underwater creatures because the water was so clear. The further we walked out into the water, the bigger the fish were, but they never bothered us. Taking a ride on jet skis was a true adrenalin rush! The entire trip was the most relaxing and peaceful experience I have ever had, and doing it again was on my list of things to-do aside from visiting Star Island with my girls.

I'm also not crazy…my husband really pushed himself to make sure I enjoyed this trip. When he fell asleep, he slept so hard, I had to check him several times to make sure he was breathing. Since I didn't want to mess up our much needed vacation, I didn't mention my thoughts and concerns, but we were going to discuss it as soon as we returned home. Especially Dr. Weiss's call that he claimed was nothing that couldn't be handled when we returned. Wait until he finds out that I will be going to his appointment with him…oh yes, I will be right there to hear from the doctor himself what is going on.

Our final night on the cruise was spent walking along one of the decks, stopping to see how beautifully the moon reflected off of the ocean. It could not compare to the pictures or even the movies we saw with the same view. Oh the handiwork of our God! No one could tell me that God does not exist just looking at everything around us.

"Did you enjoy yourself this weekend?" Gary asked me, snuggling me from behind.

"Yes…I want to do it again, maybe a different cruise?"

"We can…" was all Gary said.

"We can? You don't sound so convincing," I told him, trying to turn around to look into Gary's eyes.

"Woman, stop moving while I'm comfortable," Gary chuckled. "I just meant that we can go anywhere you would like to go on our next cruise…as long as it's just us and no kids."

"Don't you think our daughter would enjoy a trip like this? She probably feels like she's outgrown Disney or any other kiddie themed park."

"I'll think about it…in the meantime, we'll concentrate on spending more time alone together. How does that sound?" My husband asked me while slightly biting my earlobe.

"Sounds good, but it will be better when I see it happen, Mr. Workaholic," I joked, but I meant it.

"I'm planning on taking advantage of my vacation going forward because I need to do that. The guys are in their freshman year of college, and in six more years, Monét will be headed that way too…"

"I don't even want to think about being in that house by myself," I said, cutting Gary off.

"Monét talks about college now, but she says she doesn't want to follow her brothers to the college they're attending, she wants to choose something different.

"Yes, I know, but what she wants to study seems to change from week-to-week, so I won't worry about that until she's at least a junior in high school. I just hope she doesn't grow too much more at the top, if you know what I mean."

"Baby, Monét still has a way to go with that…plus I don't want to have to buy a gun," Gary stated, squeezing me a little tighter.

"You'd better come to terms with the fact that your daughter is becoming a young lady. I have to take her to be fitted for bras when we get back so she doesn't end up having problems because she's so top heavy…shoot, she's getting a little thick around her bottom too, and you can fault your genes for that," I commented.

"Sweetheart…you ain't that little back here yourself, so you can't just blame my genes…hey! I'm just joking!" Gary laughed as he tried to duck my attempts at hitting him.

"Nevertheless, Mr. Simmons, your daughter is built just like your momma used to be before she gained weight…big at the top and bottom and skinny in the waist, so you'd better hurry and get your gun 'cause the boys are probably already circling."

"Her brothers will help me keep those boys in line. If I ever see one trying to talk to my daughter, there will be problems…"

Realizing the mood change once we started talking about Monét , I suggested we take one last round in the pool. Instead of waiting for my husband to respond, I pulled him by his arm as I ran to the pool and jumped in. Gary had no choice but to join me in the fun once he was able to catch his breath after I quickly pulled him under the water with me.

When Gary and I returned from our long weekend cruise, it was back to work for us both and back to school for Monét. That first week back felt like a whirlwind trying to deal with a pre-teen who felt just knew she was going to dress for 8th grade the way she wanted to without talking to me about it first. We almost left the mall without any new clothes for Monét because after an hour of going through clothing she knew was inappropriate and a poked out lip, I was about to drag her butt to the car and let her have it. I promised myself that I would watch what her friends were wearing and talk to parents to find out if the girls had their approval to show bellies and bare breasts as if it was commonplace for 12 and 13 year-olds to dress this way.

The drive home from the mall was short with Monét sitting

on the passenger side of the car with her arms crossed while she looked out of the window to avoid looking at me. There wasn't a thing wrong with her hearing because I told her that there was no way she was going to dress like the other girls in her school.

"Do I look like their mother or yours, Monét?" I asked my daughter.

"Mine..."

"That's exactly right! Do you see me dress that way, or have I *ever* allowed you to show your body other than in a swimsuit?

"No, but Mom, you're old!"

"Girl, don't make me come across this seat on you! You're going to wear age appropriate clothing, that's the end of this discussion," I declared. "Oh, and by the way? Your mother is not old."

Monét's frustrated sigh was the last thing we heard on the ride back to the house. She grabbed her bags and hurried to her room, making sure she didn't stomp because the last time Monét decided to do that, it did not end so well for her. Our talk wasn't over because this sudden change in what she wants to wear has me concerned.

As soon as I was trying to figure out what to fix for dinner, the phone rang. The last name I expected to see on the Caller I.D. was Dr. Weiss's when Gary was supposed to have called him back when we returned from vacation.

"Hello?"

"Hello, this is Dr. Weiss. I've been trying to reach Gary Simmons."

"This is his wife..."

"Mrs. Simmons, will you please have your husband call the office and tell them that I'm requesting that he come in right away? The receptionist knows to give him an immediate appointment."

"I can do better than that, Dr. Weiss; I can make that appointment and make sure my husband comes to your office."

"Well, in that case, I'll transfer the call to the receptionist and ask them to assist you."

Once I made the appointment for the next day, I could not

wait until my husband came in from work to inform him where we would be the next day and for him to talk to his daughter before she got on my last nerve. Needless to say, Gary and I were sitting in Dr. Weiss's office the next evening listening to the devastating news that the cancer had returned.

"What is the next step?" I wanted to know.

"Well, we want to re-visit the scans and then plan from there since we have no idea whether it is in an isolated place or…"

"Or it's spread?" I asked, cutting the doctor off. I was angry with Gary because he had not said a word.

"It's possible, but let's remain hopeful that it hasn't and talk about what we will do once the scans are completed…"

"I do not want radiation or chemotherapy; I just want you to know that now," Gary finally spoke up.

"We're not talking about that at this point, we want to pinpoint where it is and the circumstances and then make such big decisions as that, Mr. Simmons."

"You're not going to just give up either," I spoke to my husband through clenched teeth. He avoided my eyes and continued asking the doctor questions until it was time for us to head home.

I could not wait until we reached the car so I could let Gary have it, but before I started good, Gary reached over to stop me my placing his right hand firmly on my left thigh and said, "Baby, it's in God's hands…let's leave it there." I couldn't even pretend that I didn't know what that meant, so I didn't say another word about Gary's health or anything else for the entire ride home. It's in God's hands.

Chapter Twelve

GARY, JR.

I was going to ignore the knock on my dorm door, but then I heard Gerald's voice on the other side. Untangling my legs with the girl I met last night, I went to the door and cracked it enough to see my brother standing there.

"Yo, G, don't miss that class this morning. Just because your grades are good doesn't mean your attendance isn't just as important."

"I gotchu, Gerald, I'm up. I'll catch up with you this afternoon before practice aiight?"

"Oh, and Mom said call her sometime today since she hasn't heard from you in a few weeks."

"Yeah, yeah, cool I'll call," I said, closing the door in Gerald's face.

"I'm calling in 20, so be up and on your way to class when I do!" Gerald yelled through the closed door.

Ignoring him, I started tapping the girl whose name I couldn't remember at the moment, so she could vacate my bed and get moving. I had to sneak her out, so she had to get a move on.

"You gotta get up...hey!"

"You need to call me by my name if you want me to do

something," the girl said, turning over looking up at me with sleep-filled eyes and a croaky throat.

"Look, you gotta go, whatever your name is..."

"Whatever my name is? Are you kidding me right now? Just in case you didn't know, my name is Katashamika! Do you know it now?" she asked, twisting her neck from side-to-side.

"Well get yo ghetto..."

"No you didn't! You don't ever have to worry about me coming back to your room, so forget my name and don't speak to me when you see me again. Humph!" Katashamika told me, forcefully pushing the blanket back and standing to her feet. "Where're my clothes?"

"You're asking me like I was the one who took them off and threw them wherever," I said, dismissing her as I gathered my shower bag and towel.

"Glad I didn't give you none 'cause you would be all childish and tell your little football friends all about it."

"Girl, please! You ain't nothing to write home about, so why would I tell my friends? You just trying to get one of us to secure your future and I've got sense enough to know when I meet a leech. So get your stuff and get out...let's go!"

"Look, I ain't trying to get caught up in here, so shut up and let me find my shoes...dang! I can't stand you!"

"Take your shoes with you...let's go," I said, leading Katashamika to the door. "Oh, I remember now why I wanted to get with you...still ain't worth all this drama though."

"Oh, you know you want *allllllllll* this," Katashamika responded by dropping down to the floor and wiggling her big butt all the way back up.

After I checked both ways before letting my guest out of the main suite door, I quickly headed for the showers so I could make it on time to my English class. I have to keep my grades up because finals will be here in just a few weeks and Gerald and I will be going home for Thanksgiving. There is no way I want to try to explain to my parents that I couldn't find my way to class for some girl.

Gerald and I met up to grab a bite to eat before he headed

off to basketball practice, and I went to football practice. Before we could make it to the table with our trays, Katashamika and a crew of her girls were headed straight for us.

Before they made it to our table, one the girls in the group said, "Uh uh, girl, you didn't tell us it was two of them. Which one did you have?"

Gerald started to leave the table, but the same girl put her hand in his chest and told him not to take another step, licking her lips, looking at my brother from head to toe and back again.

"Gary, get your girls," Gerald said, looking like he was afraid to move.

"Natasha, or whatever your name is, get your girl...matter fact, all of y'all need to go, ain't nothing here for none of y'all."

"Oh, so what you trying to say? First of all," Katashamika started, clapping her hands after each word, "Ain't nobody even checkin' for you!

Gerald looked at me and made his exit and left me to deal with Katashamika and her crew. Instead of staying there listening to her clap her hands between each word that came out of her mouth, I followed my brother and left the girls calling after us.

After that scene with Katashamika and her girls, I decided I'd better buckle down with my classes so Gerald wouldn't have to keep checking on me, and make sure I handed in my work on time. But since I kept putting my mother off, she decided she would call me.

"You can't call your mother just to say 'hello,'" she stated when I answered the phone.

"Hey, Mom, I've been really busy...you know, classes, football..."

"Girls. I've been to college, so trust me, I know there has to be a girl or two that has caught your eye," my mother insisted.

"Not really...so how's things?"

"Things? Okay I guess...but your father and I have something we need to sit down and talk to you and your brother about when you get home for Thanksgiving. Gerald told me you have to go right back to school to finish finals before you come home for Christmas break."

"Yes…I'd rather finish up the finals and come home until next semester, but I'm working hard, Ma. I know that's why you wanted me to call."

"I also miss my sons who are all grown up, if that's all right with you."

"We're not even that far away, and besides, isn't it defeating the purpose of being on our own if our mother checks up on us?"

"It doesn't matter how grown you get, as your Mom, I will always check up on all three of my kids," my mother chuckled. "You'll understand one day when you get married and have children of your own."

"I hear you, Ma. I've got to go, ok? I'll see you soon."

"All right, love you!"

"Love you, Ma!"

As soon as I pushed the 'end' button on my cell, Erica mushed me upside my head and called me a "momma's boy."

"Girl, please! Why do you think she was calling me? I ain't no momma's boy, you need to know that." Right…like I would ever admit to anybody that Mom's was my girl for life.

"Anyway, Gary, what's up?" Erica asked, moving closer to me on my bed so she could slide her Trey Songz cd into my cd player. "Yeeeeeeeah, this my song!"

"Look what the girl done did to me…she done cut me off from a good, good love…she told me that those days were gone…" Then the words seemed to ring loudly in my ears, *"…that I can be just friends with you…"* I looked over at Erica as she started loosening the buttons on her blouse and tried convincing myself that we were not friends, much less lovers, so why not get what I could get.

I met Erica about a week prior under the tunnel that connects the University Lincoln Center South and North. Students hang out at the tunnel to get a little party on with music, a little weed and meeting each other. When I saw Erica, I was like, "Dang!" She must have just come from a game or cheerleading practice because baby girl was wearing that uniform. The skirt was short enough to get my imagination working, wondering what was underneath it, and the sweater tight enough to see her breasts begging to be released from the bra she wore. Her pecan tan complexion looked extra shiny and healthy, and her eyes... they looked to be a mixture of gray, blue and hazel, all playing around with each other giving off a mysterious look that I just had to get to the bottom of.

Erica was not like a lot of the girls that attended our school. What really made her stand out to me was that it seemed to be an aura of peace surrounding her; a natural peace that felt tangible enough for me to reach out and touch. And yet, there was something wild just under the surface that attracted me to her. I had to see what she was about, so I introduced myself and we had been talking ever since.

We planned this night in my dorm room, but I never told her it would be my first time having sex. I was nervous as all get out, but it didn't stop me from catching a ride with one of my boys so I could get a small box of condoms.

Convincing myself further that it was time for me to become a man according to the definition of my friends, I pulled Erica to me and helped her take off the blouse. Watching her breast spring to life as if they had a special message just for me caused me to get a little anxious, so I kept reminding myself that this was a one-time thing and like Trey Songz was singing, we can't be friends...not after this.

I watched as Erica decided to give me a slow strip tease dance to the music as she removed the remainder of her clothing. My shirt was removed somewhere during the dance and my pants followed right behind it. Reaching over into the nightstand drawer, I grabbed for the condoms I knew were there, but I couldn't find them. I got up to get a better look, searching through the things I had there but came up empty.

"Yo, my condoms are gone...I know nobody could have gotten in here to get at them," I said, scratching the right side of my head. I bent down to see if they might have fallen out the drawer and under my bed, but when I stood up, Erica had unrolled some condoms in different colors.

"Pick a flava, baby, so I can taste it with you in it," she teased.

"I'd rather use my own…"

Moving closer, Erica put her breasts in my face, smothering me with them. It gave me a chance to inhale the strawberry scent she wore on her skin and immediately I was more than ready. Slowly we began our dance to the bed with Trey Songz singing in the background and my mind racing trying to remember the things my friends talked about in the locker room. But when Erica told me to lay back, a bad feeling flooded me and I started to stop her, but I had come too far to turn back.

"You're going to have to lose those boxer briefs if you want to get the ultimate loving that only Erica can give you…and you still haven't picked a flava," Erica told me, pointing to the different colors she held in her hand. "Cherry is my fav, so I can pick it if you want me to."

Again a feeling of dread hit me and I had to know what happened to the condoms I bought. I asked, but Erica kept telling me not to worry about it because she took care of them. But when I happened to turn my head to the right, I saw the box of condoms in the trash can that was not too far from my bed. I pushed Erica back and got the box out of the can, but what was at the bottom of the can caused me to become immediately enraged with anger. At the bottom of the trash can lay every single condom from the box, all cut up. She had to do it when I was on the phone with Moms, but how did I miss this?

"You know what? I knew something didn't feel right about this whole thing. This is the game you like to play, huh? What, yours got pin holes in them, Erica?" I walked toward her, nostrils flaring and the tips of my ears searing hot.

"What are you trying to say? I'm trying to sabotage you or something?"

"There it is…I don't care where you go, but you gotta get on up out of here," I told Erica, handing her her clothes with one swift move.

"Hold up! I don't share my special condoms with everybody; you should consider this a privilege," Erica declared.

"You ain't doing me no favors, so get your clothes on and get on up outta here. I'm done. Just the fact that you don't share them with everybody tells me you've been with some of everybody...I don't know you like that, bird!"

"Bird? *Bird*? No...you...*didn't*! Don't get mad 'cause you still green. Worse than a female tease."

"Oh word?" I opened the door wide, allowing anybody that was sitting in the common area of the dorm suite to see Erica half naked. "Get out!"

"So you're gonna do me like this? That's cool, I ain't even beat for you!" Erica screamed in my face on her way out of my dorm room, fastening her pants. "Y'all boy a old maid, scared to get a little..."

Erica's comment was met with comments and loud hoots from my dorm mates and their guests. I went back inside my room and slammed my door on all of it. I'm done trying to get with any females on this campus; Mikki's the only girl for me and I can't wait to see her during the Thanksgiving break.

By the end of the week, Gerald and I was all packed waiting on Michaela to pick us up. Since she went to Temple and her brother, Mike, registered her car in his name, she was able to have a car at school her freshman year. Mike was a sophomore and didn't want to have to be responsible for driving Mikki anywhere, especially at school.

As soon as I saw Mikki's 2007 four-door Sapphire Pearl Honda Accord coming around the corner near the Athletic dorms, I was ready to hop in and go. By the time Gerald and I placed our bags in the trunk, I closed it and found myself face-to-face with Erica. She no longer looked as good as she did to me at the tunnel or in my dorm room. I was heated immediately.

"So you're gonna leave without at least apologizing to me for the other night?"

Instead of answering her, I made my way to the front passenger seat of Mikki's car with Erica on my heels.

"Oh, this is the girlfriend? Did you tell her I let you unwrap this special present? Huh? Tell her, Gary, let her know you almost had the special privilege of tasting one of my flavas," Erica insisted, with a twisted look on her face.

"Yo, you need to move, aiight? Ain't nobody playing." I spoke calmly, trying not to explode on Erica. The last thing I needed was for Mikki to think I was cheating on her.

Gerald walked around to the passenger side of the car and asked me if I needed some help with anything.

"Two of y'all? Do both of y'all wear a skirt?" Erica asked, laughing hysterically by herself. "Wow, unbelievable!"

Gerald tapped my left shoulder and told me to just get in the car and leave Erica standing there making a fool of herself. Before I could open the door to get in next to Mikki, Erica was evidently upset because she was not receiving the action she'd hoped for.

"I...ain't...beat...for...you...lit-tle...girl!" Erica screamed, clapping her hands between each word. I have never been able to figure out why some girls do that.

"Just pull off, Mikki; this chick is crazy," I told my girl. She hesitated for a second and then pulled off, not saying a word until we were well on our way back to New Jersey.

"Who is she, Gary? Don't lie," Mikki finally said.

"I met her at the tunnel at school. She tried to kick it with me and I ain't give her none, so she called me an old maid, trying to embarrass me in front of people."

"Hmmmmm..."

"What? I'm still the same guy when I saw you last. I ain't trying to be with nobody but you," I explained. Gerald cleared his throat and asked if we could stop at Mickey D's on the way.

Michaela didn't say another word to me until after we left the restaurant and made it to I-95. "You're telling me that nothing happened between you and that girl?"

"I'm telling you the truth...nothing happened. Why do you think she was out there trippin' like that? Girl was all aggressive trying to get with me, but I know what I got at home," I assured Mikki. "Ain't like none of those nuccas on your campus ain't trying to holla at you."

"Don't try to flip this, Gary! I pull up on campus and watch some random chick come walking up to my car and act like she had a right to be all up in your face. I don't know any female that would make a fool out of herself in public for nothing unless she's really crazy."

"No worries, Mikki, his team mates been gettin' at him

all week about that same girl calling him an old maid," Gerald yawned. I knew it wouldn't be long before he fell asleep.

"For real, Gerald?"

"Yup!" Gerald said around another yawn. That would be the last time we heard from him until we got home.

"So then, there's been nobody?

"How many times can I tell you? I love you and only you, Girl."

"You better, Boy," Mikki smiled in my direction. We were cool, and all was grand in my world. That is, until Gerald and I walked in the door.

Chapter Thirteen

GARY, SR.

"Baby, they should be pulling up soon, sit down and relax."

"I'm so nervous…you know how Gary Jr. reacted the last time. This is not going to be easy," Tonya turned her worried eyes to me.

"Come on and sit beside me and we'll worry about that once the guys get here. I can't believe we agreed to let them ride back with Mikki," I said chuckling.

Once Tonya sat back on the sofa with me, I leaned my head back and closed my eyes and started humming my favorite Gospel song, "God Is," by Rev. James Cleveland. It wasn't long before Tonya began to sing softly along.

"God is my protection…Goooood iiiiis….my allllll and allllllllllll…"

I continued to hum, and my baby continued to sing. It gave me complete peace in my spirit and a confidence that only comes from knowing that God can do anything but fail. Whatever He decides to do is all right with me.

"God is my today and tomorrow…Goooooooood my God is…my all and all…"

By the time we heard to guys coming through the front door, the song was coming to a close. I held my wife tighter as she sang: "*God is the joy and the strength of my life, He moves all pain, misery and strife; He promised to keep me, never to leave me; He never, never comes short of His Word...*"

"The lovebirds are at it again, G," Gerald smiled when he and his brother walked in on us.

"They singing a duet too...Dad can only hum 'cause we all know he can't hold no note," Gary said, causing us all to laugh.

Before long Monét came running down the stairs to her mother's warning about running in the house, much less down the stairs.

"Look who it is, my book end brothers," Monét teased, ignoring Tonya.

"Pest know she misses us, Gerald," Gary Jr. countered. "Trying to grow up and stuff; I bet not see no boys trying to creep up and around here or it's gonna be problems. Tell her, Dad."

"That's right..."

"Oh, it's right, trying to get me to buy little skimpy shirts for school," Tonya added, interrupting me.

"If everybody's going to gang up on me, I'm going back to my room to finish hearing what Dana had to tell me. Be glad I came down here to see you two pains!" Monét told the guys as she tried to run back upstairs.

"No, come back here, young lady; your father and I need to talk to all of you before we sit down to eat," Tonya told our daughter.

"Aw, man! Dana has something to tell me that happened in 6th period today," Monét complained, but returned to the den so we could talk.

"What's up, Pops?" Gerald said to me after he sat on my right side. Why are you wearing a Yankees' cap in the house? They lost the series, it's over old man," he joked.

"Yeah, my boys didn't pull it out again this year, but there's always next year."

"Come have a seat Gary and Monét; I want to put dinner on the table..."

"Can't we have some pizza?" Monét wanted to know.

"Do you have some pizza money?" Tonya asked her. When

there was no response, my wife turned to me and nodded slightly letting me know it was my turn to tell our children what was
going on with me during the time they were away at college.

I turned to my children, looking them in the eye, one by
one, and finally removed my baseball cap to reveal my completely bald head. The total silence that followed was almost
eerie, and finding my voice was difficult, but I had to say something.

Explaining that the cancer returned and spread was one
thing, but it was hard to convince Gary Jr. that we would fight
this disease and win with God's help and chemotherapy; a drug
called docataxel or Taxotere ™. If this doesn't work, there are
others that we will try to beat it with our faith buried in God,
trusting Him for all things.

"Daddy? Are you afraid you're going to die?" my baby
girl asked.

"At first...but the only fear I have now is leaving here and
not seeing you grow up, all of you get married and have kids
of your own. No matter what, I trust God to do what He sees
fit...I'll be with you always in your heart. Do you understand?"

"Yes...but we will see you again...right?"

"Stay with God, and we will surely see each other again.
But today, we're talking about your dear old Dad living! We're
not defeated, do you all hear me? Gary? Gerald? Do you have
any questions you want to ask?"

What I told Monét seemed to satisfy her, but Gary Jr. sat
with his arms folded and he had dropped his head. Normally I
would tell him to pick his head up, but I knew it was his way of
hiding his true emotions. Gerald sat up on the edge of the sofa,
faced me and said, "I'm joining my faith with yours, Dad."

"Thank you, Son. That's all I ask of you...God has the last
say in the matter. Now...I don't know about the rest of you, but
I'm a little hungry. When I take the treatments, by the next day I
can't keep anything down and I feel like I've been hit by a Mack
truck. But I'm making it, so let's go eat."

Tonya went ahead of us to make sure everything was heated and ready to serve, Monét went back up to her room and I
was left with my sons. Still, there was complete silence and I

couldn't stand it; never could.

"How's school going, fellas?"

"We have to finish finals when we go back, and then we're home for good until spring semester." That was Gerald speaking for the both of them. Was a time Gary Jr. spoke for the both of them because Gerald had a hard time expressing himself. Suddenly the roles have changed.

"Sounds good! Looking forward to the holidays. Just hope we get through this one with your Auntie Denise coming for a visit."

"Hey, dinner's ready, and I heard that Gary!" Tonya called from the kitchen. "Call Monét down, will you please? And tell that girl I better not see a phone attached to her ear or I'm taking it for a week!"

Once our family was seated at the dining room table (Tonya's idea for our sons first night home), the usual family chatter started with the exception of my oldest son. He spent the entire time pushing his food around on his plate, taking a few bites here and there. Gerald, unfortunately for Monét, teased his sister mercilessly. Neither Tonya nor I stopped it; we just enjoyed the moment.

"I'm going to go to my room," Gary informed us, not making eye contact with anyone.

"Do you mind if I come up in a little while?" I asked my son. "I need to talk to you."

"Yeah...I mean, yes, Dad," my son sulked away from the table, headed upstairs to his room.

"Guess that's my cue. After I talk to Gary, I'm going to lay down a bit."

"You're not going to wait around for Denise? She said she had something to tell me once she got here. Lisa's coming by as well. She should be finished helping her mother preparing desserts for Thanksgiving by then."

"No, Tonya, I'm a bit tired...I'll talk to our oldest and then I'm in bed for the night."

I dreaded talking to Gary Jr. because I wanted him to fully understand that we're not in control of our lives. Do I want to live a long time? Of course! But as much as I want to encourage my son and help him through this period, I need the same help myself.

"Good night, family…Monét, don't be on the phone too long tonight. Dana will either be over here over the weekend or you will be at her house. You have a habit of not clicking over, Baby Girl, and sometimes there are missed calls. Hear me?"

"Yes, Daddy…you can take your cap off now that we know. You can rock a baldy for sure!"

"Thank you, Baby Girl," I said, kissing Monét on the forehead. "You may have changed the subject, but it doesn't change not a word I said to you."

"Yes, Dad…I promise."

Leaning over to kiss my wife on the lips, I made my way to Gary's room. I heard the music by the time I made it to the top of the stairs, so I know he wasn't going to make this easy for me. Perhaps the song of choice gave voice to how my son was feeling. I wanted to ask him what he knew about the Manhattans… but there was no other answer than Cecelia Simmons.

I was greeted at Gary's door with the mournful and soulful sounds of the song, "Hurt."

"Huuuuuuuuuuuuuuuurt, to think that you lied to meeeeeee…huuuuurt, way down deep inside of me…"

Chapter Fourteen

TONYA

Things were not exactly normal in the Simmons' household, but now that our children know what was going on with their father, I was able to breathe a sigh of relief and get started on our Thanksgiving preparations. I had been chopping, cutting and seasoning something all day, and I couldn't wait for my mother to come so she could take over from where I started. Thanksgiving was the next day, but I couldn't help but to feel anxious knowing that Gary's mother would also be in attendance. She had started making impromptu visits once Gary told her the cancer had returned and we had to fight a little harder this time. Cecelia Simmons was going to make sure I was doing right by my husband or there would be consequences...why I was bothered about what she could possibly do just added to my anxiety. The woman acted as if it was my fault my husband has cancer or could have prevented it.

By the time I put the five pounds of cube-cut, white potatoes in a large bowl, the doorbell rang, and I was sure it was my mother. To my surprise, it was Denise and Lisa together...Lisa left her children with her parents so she didn't have to be bothered. Since she moved back home, she craved breaks from them whenever she could. Finding a job was just another problem

Lisa was having, particularly when her main goal was to work, save money and move out of her parents' home.

"Come on in here! I wasn't expecting either of you for at least another hour," I greeted my friends, kissing cheeks and taking coats.

"Where are my handsome nephews and Miss Monét?" Denise inquired. "I know they're breaking hearts on that campus. I don't know how many little hot tails I had to straighten out when Amir was in school."

"I know Gary is talking to Gary Jr., and Gerald is probably in his room working on something. School never ends for him...now Monét? I think the phone is a permanent fixture on her ear and she has the nerve to think we're going to get her a cell phone because all of her little friends have one."

"You don't worry about her being out somewhere unable to contact you or Gary?" Lisa asked.

"No, not when I know where she is..."

"You know when we were kids we always tried sneaking off somewhere we had no business being," Denise reminded me.

"No, don't even try it! That was Sasha and Lisa because I had a curfew, thank you very much," I laughed.

"You already know Momma H ain't ever played about Tonya being out past a certain time," Lisa told us. "Shoot, I was scared of Poppa H because he would tell you he was praying for you and made you feel like you had to tell him everything you did wrong."

We all had a good laugh about my parents and my upbringing, but we still had a lot of good memories growing up finding out we were not grown at the age of 16; we just thought we were.

"Oh wait, Denise, you told me you had a surprise for us. What is it?"

"Tonya, you need to sit on down for this one because had I been standing when I received the news, I would have passed out."

"Anybody want something to drink before Denise drops this bomb that I need to sit down for?" I asked my friends.

"We can drink afterwards, I've got to hear the news Denise has for us…shoot, any news is better than listening to my soon-to-be ex-husband whining because he doesn't want a divorce and he wants me and the kids to come back home. Humph, please! I told him to stay with his little slut med student and only call me when the child support and alimony checks are in the mail."

"Dang, Lisa! I thought you were just here long enough to teach Brian that old dogs can learn new tricks," Denise commented.

"That was the problem, he learned some new 'tricks' uh, if you know what I mean," Lisa said laughing to hide her pain.

"No, I want to hear what Denise has to tell us. Let's go woman, before one of my children come down here."

"Children my foot!" Denise said as she stood up, peeking to see if anyone was coming for real. Then, standing in front of me and Lisa, she pulled her shirt up to reveal the bomb she was ready to drop on us.

"You have got to be kidding me!" Lisa screamed. I couldn't say a word at first. "Get over here and let me feel this stomach, and look at that ugly dark line running down the middle. You know you about old as dirt trying to bring another life in the world, with Amir already a grown man. Wooooo hooooo! We're going to be new aunties!"

When I finally found my voice, the only thing I could ask was how far along Denise was…and just what did Amir say, or did she even tell him.

"My grown behind son told me that was between me and whoever and he was not signing up to babysit in any way," Denise explained. "I guess he forgot how his little hard head could be when he was growing up.

"I'm just floored, Denise…a baby? Now?"

"It ain't like I planned it, Tonya. Please don't start that judgmental stuff, okay?"

"No, that's not what I'm doing…I just…I couldn't imagine at our age having another baby, that's all."

"You think I imagined this?" Denise pointed to her belly. "That's what I get for messing with a virile young man who, by the way, doesn't want anything to do with our child. I should have come back here and got pregnant by my baby daddy; he would have gladly taken care of our baby. Shoot, if only I was really going through menopause instead of peri-menopause, I wouldn't be in this situation."

"Girl, you know Tyree ain't even thinking about you with a wife and kids he's taking care of," Lisa stated. "How old are his and Elaine's children anyway? And I told you to make sure you knew what was going on with your body…now you're having a change of life baby," Lisa laughed.

"Well, you know I didn't think it would ever happen for them since she waited until she might not be able to have any…"

"And you're talking?" Lisa asked. "You know you messed up when you refused to get with Tyree. He's a good, hardworking man taking care of his family…"

"Oh, I can get him back whenever I want to," Denise cut Lisa off. "Understand that I'm the only one who has his son… Elaine has three girls and…"

"He takes care of them and you're jealous right now you don't have it…"

"Oh no, Ladies! Not in here tonight! My husband hasn't been feeling well, and we're getting ready for the holidays. No arguing, no disagreements…just agree to disagree and let it go," I stated firmly.

"Auntie Denise!" Monét screamed, running into the den. "I've missed you! And can you please tell my Mom I need a cell phone? Hi Auntie Lisa."

"Hey Miss Monét Boo! Look at you trying to grow all up… come give me a hug and kiss!"

Lisa rolled her eyes and looked at me as if Monét didn't do the same thing to her when she returned home. I can't help it if my soon to be teen is easily bored with anything that is no longer new; Lisa's being here has definitely become old to my daughter. Monét is more like Gary's mother than I'd like to admit, even down to clothes. We still have our little tit for tats in the morning over what Monét will leave the house in, and right now I believe I'm winning. However, I am far from crazy if I think she doesn't figure out a way to wear what she wants in school. Lisa never had a problem doing that. The memory of it makes me smile and I tune in just in time to hear my daughter tell me Denise agrees with her.

"Agrees with what?"

"Miss Monét explained some very valid reasons why she should have a cell phone before her thirteenth birthday…I can't help but understand where she's coming from."

"She still won't get one until Gary and I say so…I thought you and Dana had something to talk about on the phone?" I directed towards my daughter. She knew that meant to leave the room.

"Good night Aunties! I do have to call Dana back," Monét told Denise and Lisa, kissing each of them on the cheek before running back up the stairs.

"Don't even act like you don't know how it is trying to make that adjustment from pre-teen to teen, Tonya. You've got to listen to her and at least compromise."

"I know what I will compromise on and what I will not," was my dismissive reply to Denise.

"Uh huh, keep acting like you don't know and…"

"She'll come in the door with what Denise has," Lisa commented.

"No she won't, I will not entertain thoughts of that…between her father and her brothers, whoever he is that might try will definitely get hurt."

"How is Gary…really?" Lisa wanted to know.

"He's hanging in there trying to be strong for me. He told the kids tonight when the guys came in from school…Gary Jr. is very upset, but Gerald is hanging with him. I don't know how I'm going to comfort my children, and you know Monét has him wrapped around her finger. Whatever he tells her, she is perfectly fine with it."

"Are the chemo treatments doing any good?" Denise asked.

"I'm praying they do because I am not taking anything less than my husband making it through this last hurdle. I still cannot wrap my mind around the fact that he has prostate cancer to begin with and here it is again to wreak havoc in our lives."

"We're here for you, you know that…"

"I do, Lisa…now Denise, Girl, I don't know about you with a new baby trying to come on the scene when you should be preparing for Amir to extend the family," I laughed, doing my best to change the subject. That's when Denise dropped another bomb on us.

"Who? Oh no, I don't believe in abortions, but I certainly do not plan to raise this baby by myself. Uh uh, no! Baby daddy don't want no parts, then neither do I…I'm looking into giving it up for adoption."

"You lying," Lisa whispered.

"Who? Looka here, I have raised my baby and there is no room for another one in my life unless it's the kind I can have when I want and give back when I'm through…no, can't say I can do this again. Do you know how old Amir is? Child please!"

I was too through, so I did the next best thing. I headed to the kitchen with my two friends in tow and insisted that they help me finish my Thanksgiving preparations so we could at least create something close to happy, even if it was only from the smells of the food.

Chapter Fifteen

GARY JR

Gerald started going with our father when he had chemo treatments during winter break from school. I would help him get Dad back in the house when they returned, making sure he had a blanket and pillow to sit with us in the den. He was tired, that much I could tell, but no matter what, he'd stay right there so he could talk to us about whatever. How my Moms was able to walk around like my father wasn't nauseous a lot, or that everywhere there was supposed to be hair was no longer there. No mustache, nothing on his head, his arms or legs…and I could only imagine the other places that were bald as well. I couldn't confirm this because I didn't ask, and he only allowed my mother to bathe him.

Then there was Nana Cee, who came by every single day to get on my mother's nerves and treat my father like he was a baby. Sometimes he protested, but other days he was so weak, he didn't even bother. Make no mistake about it, when it was time for him to get into bed, my mother made it clear she was the boss in our house and Nana Cee said her goodbyes shortly thereafter. It was amazing watching those two try to be civil with one another while they both attended to my father. If I wasn't so messed up in my mind and heart, I would find it funny...but watching my father wasting away before my eyes took all of the laughter away from me.

No matter how many times I questioned God, prayed and asked Him to heal my Dad, he seemed to be getting worse instead of better. The side effects from the medicine was making him sick on top of the cancer, even changing it to something else didn't matter too much at all. Then one day, just before the new year, Dad stunned us all by telling us it was time for the treatment to stop...he would not, could not, continue to live his life like that. His life was in God's hands and whatever He decides about his life is what he will accept.

Mom cried her eyes out, and Monét was quiet for once in her life. Me? I did what I always do when I didn't want to deal with something so rough...I headed out the door in search of something...anything...to occupy my mind. Not that there was anywhere I would rather be than with Mikki, so that's where I went. One look at me and she knew something really bad was going on with me.

"Come on up to my room, G...we can talk privately there."

Things such as rules were relaxed once Mikki graduated high school. There was a time her parents didn't allow her to have male company in her room, but I was grateful for the fact that they now viewed their children as being "grown." As long as they didn't bring drugs, alcohol or babies into the house, it was all good. My parents wouldn't go along with relaxing that rule unless we were visiting after we were married, so I took advantage of spending time with Mikki in her bedroom. Besides, it was something I needed after my father said his treatments were done.

Once I explained to Mikki what was going on, she hugged me and held me for as long as I let her. I refused to cry because I was angry with my father because of his decision as opposed to being sad. How could he bail on his family like this? Doesn't he know we need him for...for everything?

"I'm not going to pretend I understand, but I'm so sorry, Gary. Do you think you might be able to convince him to continue the treatment? What did his doctor say?"

"He didn't tell his doctor yet; Dad wanted us to know his

decision…so what now? We're supposed to wait for him to die?"

"No, I don't think that's what he means, Baby…he's tired of how the treatment is making him feel. You said he sleeps a lot and he can hardly, if ever, keep food down because he's nauseous a lot. Not that I know about being a man, but I'm sure it's bothering him that his family is caring for him when he wants to care for all of you."

"Maybe…but me and Gerald, we got him. We will do whatever is needed. I'm seriously considering staying out of school for a semester so I can be here for him…"

"You know Gary Simmons, Sr. will not let that happen," Mikki told me, hugging me again. When she kissed me, I realized that I needed more than to have another heavy petting session with my girl. I needed her like I've never needed her before.

As long as Mikki wasn't stopping me, I kept going…removing her shirt, her pants, the t-shirt she wore over her bra… once the bra came off, I rolled her over on her bed and went for the lace panties she had on, but Mikki put her hand in my chest, stopping all movement.

"I've never…"

"You better not have. If I'm not sleeping with anyone else, you better be saving all of this for me."

"Do you have ummm, you know…a condom?"

It felt like someone poured cold water all over my body. Is she serious? A condom? Instead of telling Michaela I didn't have a condom because they were in a box in my drawer at school, I pretended to check inside my wallet as if one would suddenly appear.

"Man! No, I can't believe this!" I groaned, hoping my girl would overlook our first encounter without protection.

"We can't do anything, Baby…I want to as bad as you do, but I don't carry condoms. Sorry."

"Please, Michaela…I so need this…"

"Gaaaaaaaary, no," she whined as she pulled me into a hug. "I promise I'll go tomorrow and get some, okay? I'm not taking a chance on getting pregnant."

I consented with Mikki's request and settled on the fact that we could lie together in her bed with our under clothes on and wish for our first time together. I'd already made up my mind that I would be going to the nearest drug store the following day to make sure I kept a stash at home and in my wallet. We'll both try to figure out how to make love together for the first time; I know it will be my first. Unfortunately the temporary comfort with my girl never replaced the discomfort of my father's announcement. I couldn't help wondering if Dad was giving up, something he would never let my siblings and I do...

The best thing about my father not taking the treatments was that he started getting his strength back, and he didn't sleep as much. He even went back to the office a few half days over the holiday, but Dad couldn't hide how tired he would be when he returned to the house. As much as I've been angry with my father, I still admired his strength and disagreed with his decision to do all he could to get better. There are times I'm not sure if I'm angry with my father, or God, my mother for supporting him, and the members of our church who are in agreement and praying for his complete healing. Really? If that were true, why hasn't it happened already? Doesn't God do things rather quickly...sometimes?

Christmas was uneventful and I found myself getting ready to head back to school long before Gerald and I were required to be back on campus. While I was placing some shirts on the bed, Gerald knocked on the door and came in, something he did most of the time.

"Packing already?"

"Might as well get things out of the way...don't want to forget anything," I told my brother, refusing to look at him.

"Sure that's what it is?"

"Look...never mind. You wanted something?" I finally looked over at Gerald.

"No, not really, but I wanted to check in on you. You've been hanging with Mikki and we haven't done much since we've been home."

"Yeah...well...I won't see Mikki again until school is out,

plus she has to be back on campus before we do. What's up? You wanted to do something?"

"Possibly...you do know that no matter what happens, treatment or no treatment, it's up to God...right?"

"Gerald, I don't want to talk about it."

"Do you remember when Gram died and Nana was so sad, and all of those people filled the church to pay their last respects?" my brother went on as if he didn't hear what I said. When I didn't say anything, Gerald continued.

"I remember someone saying that dying was simply a part of life, a way to be present with the Lord once you have accomplished all that God wants you to do here on..."

"You think I remember that, much less believe it? Dad is only in his 40s! How can he be finished doing what he's here to do? Not having a father is just fine with you or something?"

"Calm down, G! That's not what I'm saying. The bottom line is, we don't have a choice in this matter..."

"Why did you tell Dad you're joining your faith with his if we have no choice? Why bother praying if the outcome is not going to be in our favor?"

"You know better than to question what God does, G."

"Question?" I chuckled. "Let's see...the man who helped to raise us may leave this world and I shouldn't question all that I was taught to believe? God is a miracle worker...well Dad needs a miracle... right now!"

"You're right, and that's what I'm joining my faith with... do you understand what I'm saying?" Gerald asked me.

"Absolutely not!"

Next thing I know, my father is entering my room, knocking as he walked in.

"Fellas, fellas, I can hear you down the hall."

The silence that followed wasn't surprising because Gerald and I both was determined that we were not going to be the first one to tell our father he was the topic of discussion, or more like our disagreement.

Looking from me and then to Gerald, my father seemed to be assessing the situation and smiled saying, "You were talking about me, is that right? Well ask me whatever you want to know."

"Why don't you ever complain about being in pain...are you in pain?" I wanted to know.

"Some, but why complain about something that will eventually ease once I take something for it. I'm feeling better now that I'm not taking the chemo treatment."

"What I don't understand is that, if you know it will cure the cancer, why you won't keep taking it until the cancer is all out of your body."

Gerald said, "Actually, Bruh, chemo not only kills cancer cells...it kills healthy cells too..."

"Didn't ask you...is that true?" I asked, looking my father in the eye, daring him to deny me the full truth.

"Yes, that's true. Sometimes the treatment does not work at all and that is when we trust God for complete healing, Son. That's what I'm doing right now, but I need to tell you both a few things...have a seat, it won't take long."

I sat on my bed and Gerald sat on the chair by my desk. We waited to hear what my father had to say, but I knew before he spoke, the weight of his words would stay with me forever.

"The one thing I want you both to do is to keep God first in everything you do...that is necessary in this life because you don't get another one. Now...something I never thought I would tell my sons so soon in my own life is...I want you to always look out for your Mom and your sister, whether I'm here or not. I'm sure it doesn't warrant repeating, so I will not say it again. Stay with God no matter what, and believe Him. Matters not what someone may say to you, or even try to convince you by showing you...always believe what God says in His Word, what He tells you and what He shows you.

"I love you, I want you both to know that...your Mom, Monét, Gary, Gerald...I love my family. Each of you means so much to me and as much as I want to live to maybe 100, I can only live as long as God says so. I'm not fighting against it... well, maybe a little bit...but I want you to be able to live your lives without worrying if there was something you could have done, or even something I could have done. Should the Lord decide my time here on this earth is not long...don't be angry...

please. Especially you, Gary Jr. I know that you may feel betrayed, but that's not what's going on here…"

"Then what is?" I cut my father off. "Dad, I'm so messed up in my head until there are days I'm not sure about anything anymore. Why would God take you away from us? Is it something we did, or you did, just what? Then I think about the loving God we were taught about all of our lives and it's hard for me to believe that a God like that would let this happen to you. I mean, you serve Him hard and even when we would laugh about it as kids, you get your praise on and don't even care…I just can't put into words how I feel because it's so many things all at once.

"Truth be told, had I listened to your mother and gone to the doctor yearly for physicals, I might not have had to go through what I'm going through right now. That and not ignoring certain things going on with my body…at least, when I think back now, I can recall a few things. However, the type of exam I would have needed to detect prostate cancer would have just come up in the last year or so. I certainly would not have thought to have an exam like that. African American men are encouraged to have their first prostate exam at 40 and I'm just a little past that age…which means the cancer had been growing for some time now," my father explained. It didn't matter about what could have been; it mattered about what is and I was not feeling it either way.

"You're saying maybe you should have started getting exams in your 30s?" Gerald wanted to know.

"Probably, but that's neither here nor there now. The thing is getting through this and living my best life…making sure my family is taken care of and looking forward to my grandchildren."

"But what if…" I couldn't even finish the question. I refused to give life to the words that have been in the forefront of my mind for weeks.

"Then it will be God's will and not mine," my father said with such a serious intense look on his face, I felt like he had already settled the outcome of all of this.

No one moved or said a word for what felt like hours, and

soon the walls of my bedroom seemed to be closing in on us. I grabbed my coat and said I was going down the street to Mikki's. It was the best temporary peace in the world…as in short-lived, not long, brief, not forever.

Chapter Sixteen

TONYA

Lisa's husband decided to fly in for Christmas, but was only successful in upsetting their children and just barely escaped Lisa's brothers taking him out back for a 'talk.' The ones who were hurt the most were Dawn and BJ; they didn't want to leave from their mother's presence and didn't believe anything their father told them. I warned my best friend about talking about Brian around the kids, no matter how angry she was. Now the children know that he cheated, and for the most part, Dawn is the only one who might understand what that really meant. At the age of 10, most children know a lot more than we did at that age. I explained all of this to my husband while we sat in the kitchen having a light lunch once our sons returned to school.

"Sorry to hear that Lisa and Brian couldn't work it out... those children will have a lot to figure out over the years. What's going on with Denise? I can't believe that girl waited until she was almost 50 to have another baby," Gary joked, shaking his head.

"Forty-five, Sweety...if she's almost 50, so are we," I smiled. "Denise said she's going to give the baby up for adoption as soon as it's born. I couldn't imagine doing something like that no matter how old I am...maybe I should adopt the baby?"

"Oh, no you don't; we're not raising any more babies…"

"Mom you're having a baby?" Monét asked as she walked into kitchen.

"Have you gone and lost your ever loving mind? There will be no more babies born in this house. Do you hear your daughter?" I asked Gary.

"Well who's having a baby?"

"One of your mother's crazy friends, and *your* mother is thinking about adopting it…now remember, she just said there will be no more babies born in this house," Gary commented as he got up from his chair.

"Auntie Denise is having a baby?" Monét asked excitedly. "That's so cool! I want to baby sit."

"Didn't have to tell her which crazy friend I was talking about, did I?" Gary found that point hilarious, laughing on his way to the den to watch TV.

"For real, Mom, you're going to adopt Auntie Denise's baby?"

"No!" Gary yelled from the den.

Monét and I laugh and discuss Denise's baby and what she may have this time. Still, I could not wrap my mind around the fact that my friend was having a baby at our age. She did tell me the baby was on the small side and her doctor was concerned, but Denise was glad she only had a few months left to be pregnant. Leaving the church she joined with no intentions of finding another one as if the church actually had something to do with the decision she made to sleep with someone she's not married to and unprotected. Denise was livid when I reminded her she did the same thing with Tyree and ended up having Amir. I guess the more things changed, the more they remained the same.

In the meantime, my daughter talked about some boy Dana liked and wondered if I would allow her to have phone calls from boys.

"Go ask your father and see what he says…I agree already," I commented.

"But, Mom, we just want to…you know…talk."

"You can talk in school, young lady. We're not even going to start having this conversation before it's time."

"Dana says that the boys really like me..."

"Girl, I know what they like, and so do you. I'm going to bind those breasts of yours up so maybe they can get to like Monét instead of what her body looks like," I told my daughter while I tried to keep my temper from flaring.

"Nana Cee said it's natural for a boy to love the kind of body that we have...and besides, I'm not a little girl any more..."

"I'll tell you what...keep talking about boys to me, hear?"

"Well, when can we talk about them?"

"When your father and I decide you are old enough and responsible enough to handle it...that's when!"

"Dana's Mom lets her..." Monét started to sulk.

"Do I look like Dana's mother to you?"

"No, but..."

"There are no 'buts,' Monét! For one thing, you have your own mind, and I don't give a care what Dana's mother lets her do, you know the rules in this house. You are not a follower, do you understand me? *Do you*?" I asked when Monét decided to cross her arms and poke out her lips.

"Yes, Mom..."

"Get that face in shape or I will help you. Dana this and Dana that...seems to me Dana is doing things that a 12 or 13 year-old shouldn't be thinking about, much less doing. Maybe I need to talk to Miss Dana's mother and find out if the things you're telling me is what she is actually allowed to do. I'd hate to break up such a long friendship."

"No, please don't do that! You will embarrass me," my daughter panicked.

"It would be in your best interest to make better decisions where Dana is concerned or I will step in and decide some things for you."

"Yes, Mom...just please don't call Dana's mother."

"Go on in the den and keep your father company while I finish cleaning this kitchen."

Monét happily left the kitchen and me with my concerns about her friendship with Dana. A beautiful child, with very light skin and long black hair that fell to her lower back. She's not as busty as Monét, but her behind seemed to grow over night, and I did see her talking to the boys on the block, making sure to switch extra hard whenever she walked. Dana was the oldest of three children. Her mother worked full-time and her father visited once in a while. I'm sure she's seeking the attention she feels she's not getting at home, but it will not happen at my daughter's expense. Monét may not approve, but that conversation with Dana's mother will be happening soon.

So much to worry about these days with Monét taking puberty by storm, talking about boys and always wondering how far she can go when wearing pants that I would consider too tight. On top of that, my husband told me that he could no longer take the chemo treatments; he was going to wait on God's divine healing for his life. Fear cannot describe what I feel coursing through my body every waking moment. I trust God and I believe my husband and have decided to stand with him and support his decision, but it is hard. *Real* hard. My heart agrees, but my mind runs through different scenarios every single day. How can I be a widow? Our sons just made it to adulthood, but they're still babies to me…and Monét's body is moving faster than the years can go by and I'm going to need help with her as she matures without strangling her a time or two.

Once I finished cleaning the kitchen, placing the last few dishes in the cabinets, I eased past the den, upstairs to my bedroom. As soon as I closed the door behind me, I dropped to my knees beside the bed and let the flood gates open. My tears flowed freely down my face, but I was afraid to open my mouth because a scream was waiting to unleash a fury of its own. I had no words to say to God as I cried…what could I say? He knows all things, but I couldn't help wondering if He knew what was going on in my entire body…my mind, my spirit, my body… just every part of me hurts. It's an indescribable pain that crying could never give release to. I never knew my physical heart could hurt so much.

I wiped my face and pulled myself up off my knees; I felt like my prayer, if that was truly a definition of what I'd just experienced, kept hitting the ceiling and falling right back onto me. I wanted to scream at the top of my lungs, "God, *do you hear me?*" Maybe then it would make it to His ears and He'd move on our behalf and completely heal my husband.

As I began removing the linen from our bed, Gary quietly walked in our room and stood watching me for a moment. When I turned around, he noticed my puffy red eyes and immediately pulled me into a tight hug.

"I'm trying so hard to be strong…but I'm starting to lose it," I cried into my husband's chest.

"Baby…who told you that you had to be strong? God gives us strength daily, just use what He gives and leave the rest to Him," Gary told me as he wiped my tears.

"The children are watching us and I don't want them to think my faith is wavering…"

"But they'll know you're human just like they are. We're in this fight together, okay? Look at me, Tonya…look at me, Baby…I know what we are supposed to do as Christians, but it is still all right to admit how you really feel about any situation. The chemicals were killing me and I know that, so I prayed about it and I stopped taking the treatments. Look at this beautiful head of curls I grew," Gary joked, removing his Yankees cap to show me. "By the way, I'm cutting this stuff down tomorrow to a respectable length."

"They're cute…leave them," I smiled through my tears. Gary really did look like a little boy with the curly hair that grew back after he stopped the chemo treatments.

"No way, they have to go because I'm tired of wearing this cap."

Gary never complained about the side effects of the treatment, but I know he was dealing with numbness in his feet and hands. He constantly moved his feet whenever he was sitting, and frequently rubbed his hands together, stopping to look at them as if there was something visible on them that could be removed. Gary always had a ready smile, even when I knew he was pushing through to keep us all encouraged. But his eyes always told me the truth. Where there was once fear and determination, something has replaced that and simply says, "settled" and "peace." It's like he already knows the outcome of his illness, he's in agreement with it, but he has not spoken the words to me.

"Why are you so...I don't know...you don't seem worried?"

"I'm not, Baby. Whatever God decides to do, I'm fine with it. Ideally, I want to live to be 150, see my grands and great-grands..." Gary trailed off.

"But?"

"No but, it just *is*. I know I can't explain to you exactly what I mean..."

"Try to explain it, I need to know that you're doing all you can to live, Gary!"

"You don't see me giving up, do you? I'm not laying around here waiting on death, Baby, I'm not. Still I trust God to be Who He is and do what He will with my life. That much I know you understand."

"Maybe 'understand' is the wrong word...forget it, I can't even put into words what I mean myself. I just cannot wrap my mind around what is happening to you, to us...our family. Doesn't God hear our prayers? He promised in His Word that..."

"Sweetheart, listen...God is *the* Promise Keeper, and the way deliverance comes is according to His will. Remember that and we can move on."

"But..."

"Shhhhhhh..." Gary admonished, taking me in his arms again, holding me tight. I have no idea how long we stayed that way, with my head buried in my husband's chest, listening to his strong heartbeat. I prayed and cried the whole time...I need my husband.

~~~~~~~~

Later in the day I found myself at my parents' house, sitting in the kitchen with my Mom while she made sweet potato pies. If anyone could understand what I have been trying to put into words, it had to be my mother. When we lost Gram, I thought my mother would lose her mind, but eventually God blessed her to make it through. It was a hard time for all of us, so she just had to help me understand this.

"The thing is, with Gary you are dealing with his illness. With Mom, she died suddenly and we didn't suffer along with her. Still, there were thoughts of what I could have done, or should have done...but I realize now that it was totally out of my hands. It's out of your hands as well, Tonya. God has the last say in it all."

"It's like Gary has given up even though he...hasn't, if that makes any sense at all."

"He's given it totally over to the Lord, Honey; that's what he's done. When I speak to him, that's what I sense...and he's satisfied with whatever way the Lord sees fit to heal him; this side of heaven or the other side."

"But shouldn't he be praying for his complete deliverance like everyone else? I mean, his family needs him...I want him here," I frowned. "I want to know why my husband? He's a good man, he serves God and man; Gary is committed to everything he puts his hands to, so why him?"

"Do you mean, why you?" my mother questioned. "That's what I'm hearing when you talk...why you...why not you? We have no way of knowing right now what God is going to do unless we believe the doctor's report...that Gary is not responding to treatment..."

"No, Gary has stopped taking his treatments. He said they were killing him and he wanted to wait on God for his deliverance. That's why I said he has given up, Mom" I explained with tears threatening to spill down my face. "I just can't keep trying to hold up this strong front for him and for the kids when I feel like I'm falling apart. And I'm scared..."

"Gary's not afraid?"

"He was, but now he's so...I don't know...content maybe."

"The only advice I can give you is to continue to trust God to answer our prayers and understand He will do accordingly... per His will. That's the part you must remember. And be encouraged, Baby; God knows what He's doing."

"Mom...I don't mean any disrespect, but I know all of that...I want to know what to do with how I feel. God's Word, God Himself...He's the answer, but what do I do?"

My mother did not answer at first, filling pie shells to be

placed in the oven. Once she finished that task, she walked over to the sink to finish cleaning the collard greens she had there before she finally turned around and faced me.

"I wish I could tell you that I don't know what you mean, but I do. When my mother died, I thought I would never be the same ever again. I was a total wreck on the inside...but I learned, day by day, that I didn't have to pretend that I was okay when I wasn't. Every day I faced how I felt and I told God about it on my knees. Angry, sad, depressed, fighting mad...so many emotions would flood my soul. 'What am I going to do without my mother?' So many thoughts, but eventually I was able to make it through..."

"But how?" I interrupted my mother. "That's probably the question I've been meaning to ask all along."

"It's a process, plain and simple, one that's not the same for everybody...day by day. In the beginning it's minute by minute and then moment by moment. Remember every single day to let the Lord know how you feel, just tell Him even though we know He knows...and allow Him to heal you," my mother explained, sounding like she went back to that time in her life.

"Gary's illness is in our family's face every single day, and I know you're the one taking the brunt of it all, but don't forget to ask God to strengthen you for this journey. Certainly He will. Don't try to rush yourself no matter what anyone tells you...it's your process, allow God's healing in His time."

"One thing is for sure...I now know what it means to ask God for strength. When I was a kid, I thought folks was just saying that to sound all deep," I smiled, shaking my head.

"Keep on living, Baby, just keep on living; you'll find out that asking for strength every day is needed..." Mom was interrupted by my father yelling out at the TV in the den. "That's proof of why I need it every day," she joked and we laughed.

My parents have always been my rock, my go-to when I felt that I couldn't talk to Gary. Now I have to talk about my husband which was none too easy. Well, at least with my Mom because Dad wasn't going to baby me, just give it to me straight and I wasn't ready to hear that. Especially now that my father was semi-retired from the bus company, only working part-time hours so he can spend more time at home with my Mom. Eating more of my mother's good cooking was more like it since he's gained a pouch over the last six months.

Dad's hair started graying around the temples giving him a distinguished look and he knew it, and he started taking extra care to choose suits that brought out his new look better. When I told him that perhaps he and my mother should walk around the mall like most old people their age, I thought he was going to take my head off: "We're in the prime of our lives, there will be no mall walking for us...do you hear this?" my father addressed my mother that day. "Plans are in the works for some vacation spots without kids...oh wait, our 'kid' is grown with her own." My father thought that was funny, but I told them they should take me with them so I could get away from my life.

Mom just gets better looking the older she gets...yes, she had some gray streaking through her hair as well, but Dad appreciated the little chubbiness that is a part of her. Instead of cutting her hair like quite a few of the older women in our church, my mother let hers grow and had it styled at the hair salon every few weeks or so. She would sport some big, soft beautiful curls or have it flat-ironed and styled really nice.

"Going to go home now, Mom, and make sure Gary's okay. Monét's taking care of him for me, if she can keep that phone away from her ear," I said, having spent enough time for my mother's pies to finish baking.

"She's a typical teen, trying to talk her grandfather into buying her a cell phone," my mother chuckled seeing the concern across my brow. "Don't worry, when your Dad found out you were not allowing her to have one, the request was denied."

"That little girl thinks she's slick, but I got her," I said, kissing my Mom's cheek.

"Take this pie so Gary can have some; he loves my sweet potato pie," my mother commented.

I didn't want to tell her that Gary may not even eat a full slice of her pie since he hasn't been eating well at all the last few weeks. He thought I wasn't paying attention, but I'm his wife...I know.

After I kissed my father, I got in my car but going straight home was not in my view. I just drove around our city, past my old high school, the mall, and through the park where my friends, and especially my husband and I made some great memories. I'm praying hard that Gary and I will be able to reminisce for years to come...God, if you hear me, please...I want to continue to celebrate life with my husband on this side of heaven.

Chapter Seventeen

GARY SR.

The morning I told my wife I would no longer continue the chemo treatments was the same day that I knew my life would no longer be the same. I sensed it...felt it...I knew it in my heart and soul that it wouldn't be long before my time here on earth would be done. Wrestling with God and His decision was hard, even after I informed my family and my doctor that I would no longer treat the cancer that had evidently spread. I made promises I wasn't sure I could keep, bargained with God to understand my side of things. In the end, I released my will to Him and He settled it in my being that all will be well.

My sons are back at school, but I'm going to have to call them in a few weeks so I can see them and talk to them. Not sure if I should tell anyone what I know is inevitable because I don't want to see their sad faces. My wife...Lord, my Baby! I never knew I could love another who was not blood related. Surely she's my gift from God. I've been watching her hold to her faith and the hope that God would miraculously heal me, but it's not to be the way we have all prayed it would be. Not that we don't know or have not witnessed the amazing healings and deliverances that God has blessed so many with, but we negate to think that healing and deliverance can mean that God takes us away from it all physically.

I'd just finished up a few things when I heard Monét calling me, letting me know that my best friend, Chad Jackson, was here. My body wasn't feeling up to climbing back up the steps from the basement, so I asked my daughter to send him down since what I needed to discuss with him was still sitting on the desk in my office.

"Hey old man," Chad greeted me with a brother hug. "What're you doing holed up down here?"

"Trying to put some things in order and waiting on you to get here. How's it going?"

"It's going, man; trying to adjust to my wife's pregnancy and her crazy hormones. As far as I'm concerned, this is our first and last baby," Chad half smiled.

Chad and I became very good friends, working with the men's ministry at church and our families hanging out together. He's Pastor Jackson's youngest brother, a police officer, a new husband and soon-to-be new father. We were happy he finally met someone and settled down. Tonya liked to tease him saying he can finally go home for a home-cooked meal instead of at our house.

"So how are you feeling? You look like you've lost quite a bit of weight since last week...are you eating okay?" Chad inquired.

"Between trying to find an appetite and actually eating, I don't get much in my gut...did I tell you I'm no longer taking chemo?"

Chad didn't say anything at first, just paced back and forth in front of my desk a few times, paused for a few seconds and repeated the action. I could tell he was trying to find the words to say to me without being offensive.

"Bro, are you sure that's a wise thing to do? What brought about this decision? What is Tonya saying about all of this?" came Chad's quick-fired questions.

"Have a seat and let me explain all of this the best way I can...please, take a seat, Chad."

It took a few moments longer before Chad took a seat on the black leather loveseat I keep in my office. I've always loved this space because it flowed into another room which was my "man cave;" fifty-two inch flat screen TV, a regulation sized pool table, a small refrigerator and plenty of snacks and drinks that are probably going bad since no one comes down here much anymore. Then again, I'm sure Tonya keeps an eye on things, so it's probably all cleaned out.

Looking at my best friend, I took a deep breath and told him what I could put into words and he sat there looking at me to see if perhaps I could be wrong in what I was saying. While Chad mulled over the things I told him, prayed too, I'm sure, I finished up the things I was also going to tell him concerning my family.

"Have you spoken to Pastor Jackson about all of this?" Chad asked with a look of concern on his face.

"Not yet, but we'll be meeting Friday night a little before service time...I made up my mind that I have to let Pastor know..."

"But not Tonya? I don't understand..."

"My wife is my heart, you know this; she's been hurting along with me through this journey and I don't want her to know until, you know," I attempted to explain.

"Until you close your eyes for good? Man, Tonya deserves better than that...tell your wife," Chad urged me, but I continued to disagree.

"I can't right now...besides, she knows. Tonya senses something in me but is afraid to put it into words. No worries, I'll tell her soon; just not today. Now, before we head back upstairs, there are some things I need to go over with you that I'm going to need your help with."

Everything was lined up on my desk in the order of what I believed was important. Tonya knew about the will because we did it together, but I made a few changes to it. Our mortgage will also be paid off and the amounts of the children's trust funds changed. Monét will receive beneficiary funds from Social Security, and if Tonya doesn't want to return to work, she will as well. My sons' and daughter's college funds were established long ago, so worrying about financial aid will not be a problem for either of them. My guys will finally learn how much was put aside for them, but I do not want Monét to know until her senior year of college.

Additionally, my sons will have more than enough money to buy themselves a car for their sophomore year of school, and I left advice as to how to go about it. Talk to their grandfather and make sure he is in on the purchase. I couldn't leave my mother out since I am her only child; I'm sure she would rather have me than any amount of money, but I would never forget her. She raised me by herself and deserved for me to thank her the best way I knew how. All of this was done because I was strategic in how I prepared my financial portfolio from the time began working at BAN. There is still money there that will be given to my family once I am gone.

After I finished with everything, I asked Chad to promise he would let Tonya know that all of these things were done, he looked at me as if he were still trying to figure out if I might be a bit premature in what I was doing before he answered.

"When the time comes, I'll tell her…"

"Please do me a favor and check in on her from time-to-time…remind her that no matter what she might be going through that day, my love will always be with her. Can you do that?" I asked as tears suddenly appeared in my eyes.

"I will…" Chad whispered, clearing his throat in an attempt to keep his own tears at bay.

"This is heavy, huh? Here…give me a hand so I can get up from here and go back to the den. Just one more thing, my friend."

"Anything,"

"There are letters in the top right hand drawer on my desk for my children; when you see things getting a little crazy, give them the letters. I already know Gary Jr. is having a hard time wrapping his mind around the fact that his father may not be here long…he's struggling badly, but he's trying to hold up a strong front."

"What about Gerald?"

"He's the stronger of the two right now, but when you give Gary his letter, give Gerald his as well. Tell Tonya her letter along with Monét's is in my safe under my desk. Can't have anybody finding it reading all that good stuff I have to say to her," I laughed genuinely for the first time since Chad arrived.

126

"Man, I do see a peace about you, and you haven't lost your joy," Chad told me, shaking his head. "All I can say is, I pray my faith in God is where yours is because I don't want to feel like God was making a mistake."

"You have no idea how many thoughts have gone through my mind, but I stand on the fact that God knows what He's doing and He promised that the good work he started in me will be finished until He comes…or in this case, comes for me. I am confident of this very thing.

"Before I forget, my Mom's letter is in my top left-hand drawer; she may need hers before anyone else, and no, I haven't told her and won't be. Cecelia Simmons will try to find a way up to God's throne to talk all of this over with him," I smirked, Chad laughed. He's been around my mother enough to know that if it were at all possible, she would do it.

Chad helped me back upstairs to the den where I had to lay down, but he stayed for hours talking to me and laughing at some of the crazy things we have done together, whether it was in ministry or our free time. So much of what we shared began with, "Do you remember when…" What a blessing to have had a friend who understands me and respects me enough to carry out some of my final wishes concerning my family. God has the rest.

Just before Chad left, Tonya came in and sat with us a while before she announced she would fix a light dinner, extending an invitation to our friend. He declined now that he has a wife at home for which we enjoyed teasing him mercilessly. I'd love to be here when his wife gives birth to their first child so I could rub it in about the late night feedings and diaper changes.

As soon as Tonya told me everything was ready, I groaned inwardly because it was becoming harder and harder to eat or drink. I'd do my very best, but I knew before I made my way to the kitchen that most of the food would remain on my plate. It's time to give the doctor a call and let him know what was going on so I can get additional help hydrating and nourishing my body. But today, I'm going to try to eat what my wife prepared so I can see a smile on her face.

Chapter Eighteen

GARY JR

Valentine's Day weekend, Gerald and I found ourselves headed home for the weekend. I wanted to stay on campus and see what I could get into, but when Dad sent us both a text asking that we come home, we had no choice. Well, we did, but Gerald insisted that we honor our father's request as if we wouldn't get to see him some other time. Thankfully Mikki was going home this weekend or we would have had to ask Mom to pick us up.

Things with Mikki have cooled down quite a bit, probably because we both are caught up with school and all that entails, but I couldn't help but sense a distance between us. True, I've kind of wandered, but I didn't sleep with any other girl and I dare not ask Mikki to avoid an argument. We slept together before we returned to school for spring semester, and it was if things changed drastically.

Unbeknownst to us until we got home, Dad had spent a few days in the hospital because he had not been eating too well. The doctor wanted to make sure his body was properly hydrated and even tried to talk my father into taking a few chemo treatments to make him comfortable, but he refused yet again. I had to say that he looked much better than he did the last time I saw him, and his haircut was cool for an old guy.

"Hey, what's good, young old school?" Gerald greeted our father.

"Everything's good, glad you guys came on home this weekend. I want to take your Mom out for a romantic dinner and a movie tonight," Dad told us.

"Does Mom know about this?" I wanted to know.

"Yup! She's upstairs getting dressed now, your sister is at your grandmother's house…"

"Which one?" Gerald and I questioned at the same time.

"Cecelia Simmons, my bookends," my father shook his head, smiling. Gerald and I will always have that 'twin' thing going on.

"Why did you want us to come home this weekend if you had plans with Mom? I could have gotten into something on campus tonight," I explained.

"I have brunch planned for us as a family tomorrow and I didn't want you two to be late. I figured you might have something planned with Mikki," my father addressed me.

"Nah, she only came home to study because it would be hard to do it on campus with the parties going on all weekend."

"Hmmmmmm…" father responded, tilting his head from one side to the other as if he could see what I really meant.

"Your mother's favorite restaurant, Kara's, serves breakfast now, so be ready no later than 9:30 a.m. so we can all meet there on time."

"Aren't we all riding together?" Gerald asked with a puzzled look on his face.

"We are…here comes your Mom now. Excuse me while I escort my wife to dinner fellas," my father said with a brighter smile on his face.

When my mother walked from the staircase into the den, Gerald whistled and I was speechless. Mom was looking…dare I say…hot? She had on a beautiful dark blue dress that fit her like a woman I would be checking out. No wonder Dad's smile gained some wattage when he knew she was on her way down the stairs. And when was the last time my mother put on some heels higher than two inches?

"Oh nah, Mom can't go anywhere like this!" I said before

I could catch myself.

"And why not? You don't think this is appropriate?" my mother asked me, twirling around and striking a pose.

"She's going out with me so I can show her off...you guys have a good night and we just might see you in the morning," my father smiled as he clumsily helped my mother with her coat. He didn't look too bad in his blue suit that complimented Mom's dress.

"Mom and Pops acting like they grown tonight, Gerald," I laughed. It was good to see them looking good and having fun.

"I want you to have my Moms back at a decent hour, Pops," Gerald joked.

"Yeah, and don't do anything we wouldn't do," I added, laughing.

"You two better not do *any*thing," my father jokingly threatened on his way out the door with my mother on his arm.

Both Gerald and I headed up to our rooms, and hard as I tried to find something to get into, none of my friends in the neighborhood was available. I made one more attempt to talk Mikki into spending some time, even if she came down here for once, she declined stating she was so behind with her home-work. Sounded to me she must have been partying instead of hitting the books. I left her alone and went to the den to watch TV and found myself fast asleep when my parents returned home around 1 a.m.

Mom was doing her best to try to get Dad's coat off, but he appeared to be so exhausted, so I got up and took care of it for her. I helped him make it to the sofa in the den, and he sat there with his head back, eyes closed looking like he'd been through the wringer.

"You okay, Pops?"

"Yeah...I'm tired, that's all. I'm going up in a few minutes."

I looked at my Mom, and for the first time since my father has been sick, she had worry lines on her forehead and a frown on her face. She wouldn't look at me either, just busied herself picking up things around the den.

"I have that, Mom, that's my junk. I fell asleep before I had a chance to clean it up."

"No, it's fine, I'm going to the kitchen anyway…" she told me on her way out of the den.

My father had started snoring lightly, so I went to the kitchen to talk to my Mom, but I overheard her on the phone leaving a message on my father's doctor's answering service: "Yes, this is Tonya Simmons, Gary Simmons' wife? I'm calling to ask you if we should see you in the office first thing Monday or simply go back to the hospital. My husband became violently ill tonight, and he's still not holding food or liquids down very well. Please call me back on my cell phone at…"

I walked into the kitchen at the end of the message, doing my best to pretend that I didn't hear all of the message.

"Mom, is Dad really okay?"

"I want to say yes, but he got sick at dinner and barely made it to the bathroom on his own. Thank God some of the members of our church was out for dinner tonight, and a few of the men helped him back to our table…and then helped him to the car."

"Did he drive tonight?"

"No, he hasn't driven in a while…listen, why don't you help me get your Dad up to bed so he can get the rest he needs. Now tomorrow he'll probably wake up rested and good as new. Could have been something he ate tonight that just didn't agree with him. He was doing okay after his last hospital stay, but slowly his appetite has started disappearing again."

"Don't worry, Mom, I have him. Why don't you go on up and take care of yourself for a change?"

"Thank you, Baby…I'm exhausted," my mother said, kissing me lightly on my left cheek. "I'm glad you and your brother are home this weekend."

It wasn't as hard as I thought it would be to get my father up the stairs to his room by myself since he didn't weigh nearly as much as he once did. I went to Gerald's room to wake him up so he could help me get Dad's clothes off, and those two were cracking jokes and laughing. Seeing all the weight my father really lost once his clothes were off broke my heart. However, no sooner than my Dad was comfortable in bed, his light snoring began again, and I knocked on the bathroom door to let my mother know he was fine and we were headed to bed. Sleep wasn't coming any time soon, I already knew that.

~~~~~~~

The next morning, true to his word, my father was up preparing for our brunch at Kara's. He was moving a little slow, but his smile was in place and his spirits were high; it was enough to make me overlook his appearance and enjoy the time with him before Gerald and I headed back to school.

To our surprise, not only did Nana Cee meet us for brunch, but my mother's parents along with Lisa and her crew. Dad was treating everyone to a post Valentine's Day feast and fellowship. It was cool, I had to admit. It was the best watching my father enjoy everyone and Nana Cee fussing over him while my mother appeared to ignore her. I guess this was their compromise, at least until Dad is better and his mother won't have to interfere. I noticed that my father ate a little of everything on his plate, but I kept an eye on him for any signs of the illness he experienced the night before. When we made it through the meal with no signs of sickness, I was relieved and yet again felt my hope grow a little stronger. Maybe Dad made the right decision refusing any more chemo treatments. At least until I saw Mom's face when she answered her cell phone.

Needless to say, going back to school was hard for Gerald and me both, especially when Dad told our mother he was not going to the hospital. Glad she waited until we returned home to tell him what the doctor said on the phone.

"I'm better today, Tonya. You saw that I ate more today than I did last night…and I'm drinking water and keeping it down. Call Dr. Weiss and tell him I'll make an appointment to see him next week. I plan to be in church tomorrow, so all of that will have to wait."

That's exactly what happened…we were all in church before Gramps drove me and Gerald back to school. Dad ate a pretty decent breakfast Sunday morning, praised God with an energy that his body belied, and all appeared right with our world. If that were so, why did I feel like the floor was about to disappear from beneath my feet?

Chapter Nineteen

TONYA

Gary was not pleased with me at all, but when he became so violently ill at dinner on Valentine's Day, I was so afraid that I called Dr. Weiss as soon as we returned home. I didn't care that it was late, I needed answers as quickly as possible. But I wasn't wrong…the doctor wanted him to go to the E.R., but Gary refused saying he was better. True, he didn't get nauseous when we went out to brunch with our family and friends, but it did not quell my fears that he was sick at all.

My father took our sons back to school and Gary and I stayed at home watching TV instead of returning to church for evening service. He admitted that he was tired and just wanted to rest, even opting to take a pain pill. It wasn't very often he would do that, but lately he has started moaning in his sleep. Not loud enough for the rest of the family to hear at night, but I know because I don't sleep soundly any more.

Since my husband refused to go back to the hospital, I made sure he went to the doctor that following Monday morning. My mother-in-law accompanied us, something she never did because she did not want to hear anything bad concerning her son's health. Her presence did nothing for me since I've been carrying the weight of Gary's illness the entire time.

"I'd still like to put you back in the hospital to help you hydrate quicker and to give you nourishment you're not getting from food."

"I'm eating and drinking better, doc," Gary winked. "My strength is better as well, so no need."

"You don't seem to be too steady on your feet, and that's a concern…"

"Gary, please do what the doctor suggest," Cecelia cut in. "Doctor, is my son going to live through this ordeal without the treatment? He won't tell me anything one way or another; that's why I'm here."

"That's up to your son to tell you, I cannot do that unless he gives me written permission," Dr. Weiss explained.

Cecelia looked at me, but I put my hands up to let her know it's out of my hands. Besides, I'm sure Gary hasn't told her any more than he's told me…he trusts God, and we all had better accept that because we will get nothing else. I know that Dr. Weiss said it doesn't look good and that he wanted to continue to work with my husband to help turn things around, but Gary is the one who refused. I'm hanging on by a thread waiting on our miracle from God, but my nerves are in shreds…still I put on a front that I'm totally in agreement when there is a part of me that agrees with the doctor. We don't have them for nothing.

"What I'd like you to do is to continue with the liquids and eat…and if you find eating becoming difficult, you can try Ensure ™ to keep you nourished as well. Thankfully they come in plenty of flavors today and it will also help you to gain the weight you need."

"I've given him the supplement and he's keeping that down pretty well, so I'm not as worried about the lack of appetite some days…but the weight loss…"

"Keep doing what you're doing; I'd like to see you back in a week so I can monitor your progress. If I don't see any improvement, I'm going to have to admit you. Clear?" Dr. Weiss stated.

"Oh, he's going in there," Cecelia said. "We'll do everything we can to make sure he's doing what he's supposed to do, isn't that right, Gary?"

I rolled my eyes and Gary smiled, patted his mother on the hand she had on his left shoulder and slid from the exam table onto his feet. I guess that was his answer to it all since Cecelia and I seemed to be far more concerned about his health than Gary was.

A few days later, I awoke to Gary patting me on my arm. At first I thought he was just reaching out to touch me, but when I turned over to look at him, his skin color didn't look right.

"Baby, what's wrong?"

"I'm not feeling too well..." he said, barely above a whisper. "I think maybe I should go see Dr. Weiss."

"No, you're going to the E.R. Let me call my mother and have her see about Monét and..."

"No, I don't want to go to the hospital..."

"Gary Simmons, Sr.! I am not arguing with you this morning!" I said, hopping out of bed and began pulling something to wear from the closet. Next, I called down the hall to see if my daughter was up, but she was already downstairs eating breakfast.

"Call Nana and tell her I need her to pick you up from school this afternoon."

"Okay, Mom. Do it now?"

"Yes, now, do it now, Baby Girl..."

When I went back into the bedroom, Gary was lying so still that I decided to forgo trying to get him up and ready for the hospital, I called 911 for an ambulance and then hurried to the bathroom to splash water in possible and necessary spots, brushed my hair while I put on my clothes as the sirens roared closer with each second.

"Mom! An ambulance is in our driveway!" Monét yelled up the stairs.

"Open the door and show them to my room, Baby, please!"

Surprisingly, my daughter didn't ask questions or waste time leading the EMT workers up to the bedroom. When Gary realized what was happening, he tried to fight the workers, but he had no real strength to do so. He was absolutely adamant about not going to the hospital, and I could not understand why.

"No, no, stop...please stop!" Gary insisted as the two men tried to get him up and to a sitting position. "Tonya, Honey, not this way, okay? I'm fine right here at home..."

"Baby, you're not. Please let these young men take you to the hospital. I'm going with you and you'll be just fine," I tried to convince my husband.

"Ma'am, if he refuses the ambulance, we cannot make him go. Let's check him out and see how he's doing and if he really needs to go, we will tell him," one of the attendants told me.

"Do that...check him out," I responded with tears in my eyes. That's when I realized my daughter was standing in the doorway. Immediately I went out into the hallway and closed the door.

"Mommy, I'm scared," Monét sobbed into shoulder.

"I know, I know...but your father is going to be fine as soon as we can get him to the hospital. Go on downstairs and finish getting ready for school and I'll make sure to call the school later and let you know how your dad is doing. Deal?"

My daughter looked at me with tears falling down her cheeks and dripping onto my blouse and simply told me, "I can't."

"Go call Nana and tell her what's going on and ask her to come pick you up and meet us at the hospital. Can you do that?"

Monét nodded and slowly walked down the stairs to make the call while I continued to wait in the hallway for one of the medics to come and tell me whether he believed Gary should go to the hospital. It didn't take as long as it felt when I was told my husband definitely needed to go to the hospital.

"He's dehydrated and weak...still..."

"I'm his wife, and, and he's a cancer patient...he doesn't have a choice but to go. He's in his right mind, but I'm making this decision."

When the medic looked as if he was going to protest some more, I told him that he would not get into any trouble for a decision that I made. Gary was going to the hospital and that's exactly what happened. He fussed all the way there, but I pretended not to hear him and let him blow off steam. For the first time in months he was angry, and I figured it was because his body was not getting well and that somewhere in all of the emotions he'd been experiencing, anger was there and finally having an outlet. I rubbed his hands, thanked God that my husband was going to finally get the medical attention he needed and I would be able to breathe a little bit better.

By the time Gary was treated and in a private room, Dr. Weiss stopped in to see how things were going. I was completely stressed and sat in the chair wringing my hands until he walked in to check on my husband.

"How's the patient?" Dr. Weiss asked as he picked up and began reading Gary's chart without looking at him. Once he placed the chart back at the end of the bed, he walked over to my husband and started examining him.

"Is he going to be okay?" I just had to know.

"Well, I've started a low dose of morphine ™ to make him comfortable...he's in more pain than he lets on," Dr. Weiss half smiled, and Gary cringed. I'm sure that was something he did not want me to know. "Otherwise, we will continue fluids intravenously and try to get some food in him."

"That doesn't sound so promising, Dr. Weiss. His appetite hasn't been the greatest lately,"

"Yes, I know, but perhaps once we get him hydrated again, it will improve. How does that sound? We can only do as much as Mr. Simmons allows us to do since he's refused the treatment."

"I know...I know," I told him with tears in my eyes. If Gary wasn't already sick, I would wring his neck!

Once the doctor left, Gary and I were silent until my mother and Monét came into the room. He talked to us in between the little naps he would take, but I needed to speak to my husband alone...he's got to go back on the treatments if they are going to prolong his life.

"Mom, will Dad be coming up today?" I asked my mother.

"I left him a note, so he should be or he'll call. What about my grandsons? Do you plan on calling them?" my mother asked while she checked to see if Gary was awake.

Before I could answer, Gary replied without opening his

eyes, "No...they need to go to class. I'll let you know when you should call."

That was the end of that discussion: Gary Simmons, Sr. had spoken and my mother insisted we honor his wishes and not do what we think is best for us. I didn't want our sons to be in the dark about anything, but I also didn't want my husband getting upset with me. Spring semester started mid-January and they were just at home the weekend of Valentine's Day, so I decided not to push it.

Each day Gary was getting stronger although the doctor took him off of solid foods and put him on soft foods so it would be easier for him to swallow. The doctor even talked about possible rehabilitation to help strengthen his legs because he'd been in bed and pretty much inactive for a while. I told the doctor just one thing at a time; I wanted to see my husband back home with his family before there is any talk of rehab or anything else. But what do I know? Trying to trust God while standing on what my husband has decided and listening to the doctor had my head spinning; all I wanted to do was go somewhere, anywhere so I didn't have to think.

My mother kept Monét at her house for the remainder of the week, and we made it to Sunday. Gary was anxious to get out of the hospital to at least attend church service, but Dr. Weiss disagreed. My husband was not happy about that, but if he was allowed to go, he would have had to go in a wheelchair, and I know he would have disliked that even more. I think the members from our church that took the time to come by after service brightened his day. Even more so when Pastor Jackson and First Lady Jackson stopped by to talk and pray with Gary, who joked around more than he has in quite some time. Perhaps this was the turnaround we were praying for, the miracle that I just knew God was going to give us in spite of the doctor's report.

That Sunday evening I didn't leave my husband's side until visiting hours were well over and the medication for pain caused my husband to sleep against his will. I was tempted to buy something from the drugstore to help me get some much needed rest, but the thought that I might wake up too late in the morning caused me to change my mind. Still sleep evaded me as I held onto my husband's pillow, smelling his scent…his Suede Black cologne…longing to feel his body, the security and protection that comes along with that. By the time the first rays of the sun were coming up in the morning, I was already in the shower.

Later that morning Gary was able to sit up, so I sat in a chair beside his bed, holding his hand watching talk shows and whatever else he wanted to see when he looked at me and told me he wanted me to go to work the following day.

"Are you sure? I can wait until you come home and get situated before I return. They are aware of why I'm out."

"Sweetheart, you've been out long enough. I know you have tenure on your job, but don't take advantage of it. The staff here treats me well, and I'm feeling pretty good today, so…" Gary's voice trailed off.

"So what?"

"Do me a favor and go, can you do that for me, Baby?" Gary grabbed my hand and kissed it passionately. "See? I'm all good," he said with a convincing smile.

I agreed so we wouldn't spend the time going back and forth. Besides, it's been days since I've been in the classroom and I know my students have been giving the substitutes a hard time. So that evening when visiting hours ended, I went home and slept in the den on the sofa accompanied by the TV and my favorite dark blue throw. I slept the entire night, finally getting the rest my body needed desperately. But the first thoughts on my mind that morning was what Gary said to me before he fell asleep the night before: "Always know that when God does not do things according to how we've prayed does not mean He isn't able…and He's still good, Baby…He's still good."

As soon as I walked into the front office to pick up mail from my inbox, a few of the teachers stopped to chat and ask about my husband. I told them he was still in the hospital, but coming along pretty well. The doctor did say he was looking to release him sometime this week, so we were hopeful that hospital stays would be few and far between.

Just before I walked into my classroom, I heard my cell

phone ringing at the bottom of my purse. I felt around inside my hobo styled bag and found it quickly, answering without looking at the Caller ID.

"Hello?"

"Ma?"

"Yes Gary, how are you? Everything okay?"

"Do you know that I've been trying to call Dad and his phone keeps going straight to voicemail? I figured Sunday he turned it off because of church, but now..."

"Honey, your father's in the hospital..."

"Why didn't anyone tell me and Gerald? We're coming home..."

"No, stay in school. Your father didn't want us to tell you guys because you need to finish the semester. He'll be coming home any day, so no worries. He was dehydrated and his appetite hasn't been so great, but he's fine."

"All right, Ma, all right...gotta go to class, talk to you later."

"Love you, Son."

"Yes...love you too..."

My children were so excited to see me back and it took a little doing to get them settled for the first lesson of the day, but we had just gotten into a groove when the intercom in the class rang. When I answered it, I was told that I had an urgent phone call in the front office. Taking a moment to ask another teacher to look in on my students, I half ran-half walked to the office with panic filling my heart. I prayed, *"Lord, please don't let it be about Gary...please, Jesus, please..."*

When I reached the office, I was afraid to pick up the phone, but I pushed through the fear and answered quickly.

"Mrs. Simmons? This is Shara Jackson, the head nurse on the floor where Mr. Simmons is a patient. Dr. Weiss is here and he's asking that you return as soon as possible to the hospital."

Since the nurse didn't sound anxious or sad, I breathed a sigh of relief and told her that I was on my way. I held to the sound of the nurses' voice believing that perhaps they were releasing Gary and I was summoned there to get him ready to leave. Yes, that has to be it.

Relaying my situation to the principal, I went back to the class to tell my students I had to go but that I'd be back the following morning wasn't the way I expected my first day of work to be, but it wasn't long before I was on the highway headed for the hospital. I prayed and praised God all the way...until I walked into my husband's hospital room.

"Mrs. Simmons, I'm glad you were able to get here so quickly," Dr. Weiss greeted me. No hello, good morning, nothing else.

"What's going on?" I asked, my heart thumping double time in my chest.

"Last night Gary appeared to slip into a coma...wait, let me explain. Sometimes this happens and they come right back out of it, but when I came in here this morning and found Gary in this state, I knew that there is a chance he may not wake up. That's the reason I had the nurse call you..."

"Why didn't someone call me last night? I was at home and someone could have called me and I would have been right here!" I screamed.

"I understand, but there was no need to alarm you until we knew for sure..."

"I want to know *every single thing* going on with my husband! That was no one's decision to make but mine," I broke down crying hysterically.

Dr. Weiss patted my shoulder and explained a few more things to me. My heart quivered erratically and I could hardly understand what he was saying to me. In the meantime, a nurse came into the room and checked the newest machine connected to my husband's bed that they used to clean his airway of the mucus that had started gathering there.

"Mr. Simmons's organs began shutting down, the morphine has been increased to help make him a little more comfortable..." I heard the doctor's voice trail off because I could no longer listen to him tell me my husband was dying. Instead, I walked over to his bed and hesitantly grabbed his right hand.

"Go on and hold his hand so he'll know you're here," the nurse told me with a polite smile.

When Gary opened his eyes, they were a pale gray color, as

if the very life had drained out of them.

"Mr. Simmons, your wife is right here with you," the nurse told Gary while she held his left hand.

Gary turned his head to me and opened his eyes…they were the normal brown color I've been looking at every day since we were in high school. He knew what side to look to without me saying a word because he knew his right side was my special side of him. Gary nodded and closed his eyes and seemed to relax now that he knew I was there with him.

The doctor finished writing a few things in Gary's chart and told me he would be back the following day to check on my husband. When the doctor and nurse left the room, I whispered into my husband's ear and asked him if he was tired and he whispered back… *"Yes…I'm tired…"* That is the moment my prayer went from God's total healing and deliverance to accepting His will for whatever the outcome would be for my husband's life. Still, there was a part of me that held on for that miracle I'd been asking God for.

Making the call to our family members was the most difficult thing I had to do that day. Watching them come up to the hospital and look at my husband, shake their heads, pray, sit and try to encourage me was very difficult. The only person missing was Monét because I didn't want her to see her father like that. He'd have a fit if I allowed her in there, but just before visiting hours were over, my father brought my daughter to see her father.

I expected my daughter to scream and have a fit, but she came in and laid her head on Gary's left shoulder and let her tears flow. Gary's hospital gown was soaked by the time Monét lifted her head and kissed her father's cheek gently and whispered something into his ear. Finally she looked at me and asked, "Mom? Can Dad hear me?"

"Yes, Baby…the nurse told me he can hear all of us." I didn't tell her that the nurse actually told me the hearing was the last to go. I was glad of that because I sang Gary's favorite Gospel song in his ear every chance I got when we were alone. God Is.

The following morning I was greeted by my sons as they entered their father's room, tentatively at first because they had no idea what to expect. Gerald leaned down and kissed my cheek and stood beside me looking at his father with sadness consuming his whole being. Gary Jr. stayed at the foot of his father's bed, looking on with silent tears streaking his face.

"Mom, are you okay? I know you've been here all night," Gerald commented.

"How did you two get here?" I asked instead of answering my son.

"Granddad came and picked us up last night so we can be here with you and Dad. Mom, what is the doctor saying?"

"Nothing I want to hear," I made a horrible attempt at a joke. "All we can do is wait…but talk to dad, he can hear you."

Gary Jr. made the first move. He pulled a chair up on his father's left side and held his hand. Still he never spoke a word, just let his tears speak for him. Occasionally his body shuddered, and immediately all I wanted to do was take away the pain my children were feeling. I prayed that if God didn't allow Gary to stay with us that He would take away our pain…it was palpable, tangible all around us.

Later in the day Chad stopped by because he's heard that Gary had taken a turn for the worse. It was then that he told me that he promised my husband that if anything were to happen to him, he wanted Chad to check in on me and our children. I don't know how my sons are going to take that revelation since they're all grown up now, but it was a consolation to me to know that Gary spoke to someone about what he wanted for us in his absence.

That evening I asked for a pillow and a blanket and spent the night with my husband. I pulled the chair up as close as I could get it to Gary's bed and laid my head on his chest and listened to his heartbeat. The one that matched mine perfectly, that comforted me in the night and calmed my fears. My husband… the only man I loved after my father my whole life. I love this man! How can it be time for him to go? There is so much we haven't done yet and so much we've talked about doing together once our children grew up and left home. Enjoying our grandchildren together…growing old together and walking off into the sunset together. Now a part of me is leaving and I still had a hard time wrapping my mind around it.

The following morning Gary's condition had not changed any, and his body fluids had begun backing up on him. The catheter they had in place was not ridding him of his fluids, the evidence of that building in his belly. Still I held onto my love because it was just too hard to let go. It was now Wednesday, and the only thing I did was go into the bathroom to wash my face and brush my teeth with what the nurse gave me the night before. The bags under my eyes looked like they invited some friends along, but I refused to go home to get some much needed rest. I had to be with my husband for as long as possible.

By that afternoon, Dr. Weiss returned to check on Gary's progress although I know he was briefed before he entered the room. My children had returned with my mother and we sat there watching at the TV and trying our best to talk positively so Gary wouldn't hear anything negative. But when Dr. Weiss informed me that he was doing what my husband allowed, even in this state, he would not be allowed to resuscitate him.

"Wait…what?"

"Mr. Simmons signed a living will when he was here last and on it he checked the "do not resuscitate" box, which leaves me no choice but to continue to make him as comfortable as possible. I'm sorry, Mrs. Simmons."

I ran from the hospital room, down the hall to the ladies' room so I could cry in peace. My husband made sure that no matter what, he would not stay alive a moment longer than we want him, because obviously he doesn't want to live any more. Why hadn't Gary told me about this? Right…I would have thrown a fit until he changed all of it, that's what. I was just outdone.

When I came out of the bathroom, I was met by Gerald who was shuddering as if he had been crying for hours.

"Baby, what's wrong? I'm okay…"

"Mo..Mom…it's not you. I-I-I overheard the doctor say to the nurse that Dad probably won't make it past the weekend," Gerald cried. I held my big and tall son in my arms and rocked him like he was a baby, soothing him with my words, reminding him the doctor does not have the last say. I was doing my best to soothe me too…it wasn't working so well.

Needless to say, we held onto what we could for the rest of the day, and my sleep-deprived body finally gave in to a deep slumber as I lay resting my head on my husband's chest. Although the nap was short, I dreamed very vividly about Gary. He told me that he could hear everything we were saying and he really loves us. Then he took me into his arms, kissed me full on the mouth, and began rubbing my back the way he does when I'm really upset and he's trying to comfort me. It was soothing and peace was all around me; my body began to go limp in my husband's arms. Sitting me in a chair that seemed to appear out of nowhere, Gary walked over to Gary, Jr., Gerald and Monét, and hugged and kissed each one. Then stepping back to look at us he said, "In three days I will meet Jesus face-to-face…I don't want to leave you, but I am prepared to go. I love you all… in three days." Blowing me a kiss, Gary faded into nothingness. I jerked awake and looked at my husband who had tears at the bottoms of both eyes…I could hear him crying although he never opened his mouth. I got up and grabbed some tissues and wiped his eyes and reassured him that I was there and that it was okay…he can go on and rest.

By Friday, Gary continued to deteriorate until I actually smelled a stench coming from his body. I called the nurse in to bathe him although he was bathed earlier that morning. When I stepped out of the room, I heard him say, "Okay! Okay!" That was when I realized that my husband was really in a lot of pain; he had to be for him to yell out like that when he didn't talk since the day I asked him if he were tired. I hated that he was in so much pain, and by that evening, he had begun to moan quite a bit, something he hardly ever did before.

That evening Gary's Mom, my parents, our children, Chad and Pastor Jackson had all come by to see about him and encourage me and our children. Monét was a lot better than she'd been earlier in the week, but Gary Jr. was still the one I worried about the most. He has not spoken very much at all, but he made it to the hospital along with his brother every day, as early as they could possibly get there.

When everyone else left, I washed, brushed my teeth and changed into the clean clothing my mother brought to me from my house. I didn't do it earlier because I didn't want to leave my husband's side for a second, but I'd gotten tired of wearing the clothes I'd had on for the last two days.

Again, I took up my position next to my husband's bed and laid my head on his chest and listened to his heartbeat throughout the night. I continued to sing to him, whatever song came to mind. I remembered how he loved to hear me sing, especially when I sang to him the entire night knowing that it was a comfort to my husband.

Later in the wee hours on the morning of Saturday, February 28th, I lay awake in the pull-out chair in Gary's room and thought that maybe the dream I had was just my mind working itself out. Yes, maybe that's all it was. But suddenly the heart monitor began beeping crazy and I heard footsteps running down the hall towards Gary's room. Snatching back the curtain, two nurses hurried in and began checking his vitals and the monitor just as a doctor on call ran into the room.

There was nothing else the doctor and the nurses could do but call Dr. Weiss to inform him of what was going on. I held Gary's hand and watched as his heart slowed down more and more seemingly with each passing minute. I kissed him again and again, saying, "Baby, take your rest... I'll see you soon..." But my mind was screaming, *"Baby, don't leave me! Don't leave, don't leave us please! Just stay a little while longer, just a little while longer... please!"* I knew that Gary was in a lot of pain, and even though his heart rate was slowing, he was still moaning. A part of me wanted him to let go, and the other part of me wanted my husband. I felt like two separate people fighting myself until I looked down and saw that Gary opened his eyes. Could this be my miracle I had been praying and asking God for all along? Gary smiled at me, slowly closed his eyes and he was gone the moment our doctor walked into the room.

"He just expired, Dr. Weiss," one of the nurses informed the doctor. Looking at his watch, and then checking my husband's vitals, Dr. Weiss declared Gary dead at 6:30 a.m., and I felt the blood drain out of my body.

Pulling a chair up to the side of Gary's bed, I took his hand in mine, rubbed his face and spoke to him as if he could still hear me. The doctor and the nurses left me to myself as I rested my head on my husband's chest waiting to hear his heart beat again, his troubled breathing. But it would not return, and so I lay there allowing the tears to run down my face when I could find no more words to say.

I don't know how long I was there when my parents walked through the door. Mom pulled a chair up next to mine, taking Gary's hand from me. She took me in her arms, resting my head in her healthy bosom. Humming a tune I could not make out, I could feel her hot tears falling on my bare arm. Dad said a scarcely audible prayer, and I watched him cover Gary's body with the sheet as if he were putting his son to bed. Leaving Gary's face exposed, my father rested his hand on his head and then turned to me.

"Tonya, Baby Girl, come and let's go to the house. Let the doctors do what they need to do now," Dad said.

"Dad! I can't just leave him here all alone! I mean, he... needs... me," I said with fresh tears running down my face. Even when the words left my mouth, I knew Gary would never need me again. But I needed him, wanted him with all of my soul. My heart ached so until I could hardly breathe, and the longing of my being was deeper than any I have ever experienced in my life.

Somehow my parents talked me into leaving Gary's room. Dad told Dr. Weiss what funeral home to send my husband's body to as we made our way past the nurse's station.

"Mrs. Simmons, my condolences," Dr. Weiss said, taking both of my hands in his. "My deepest, sincerest sympathies."

"Thank you... you did all you could," I said, knowing full well I didn't believe what I had just said. Leaning heavily on my father, I allowed my parents to lead me to their car, while I promised myself that I would never step foot in that hospital ever again.

Chapter Twenty

GARY JR.

No one had to say a word when my grandparents brought my mother home; Dad was gone. I knew he was going to be gone before the weekend was over just like the doctor said. I'd done a little research on Morphine and found out that it's used not only to make cancer patients comfortable, but to help usher them to their deaths as slowly and painlessly as possible. The drug is a dangerous one and I wanted to find a way to make the doctor and the hospital pay for killing my father. That's the way I felt.

When Nana Cee hit the door, her screams penetrated every wall, floor and window in the house. *"My baby is gooooooooooone! Lord have mercy on my soul, my baby!"* It was the pain that I felt through my whole body, every part of me, yet I could not shed one tear. What good was crying going to do? It wasn't going to bring my father back, so why bother? My anger only added fuel to how I was feeling and I knew that if anyone said the wrong thing just one time, there was going to be some serious problems for that person.

Gerald stayed in his room, and every now and then I would hear him cry out, but he wasn't angry, just really sad…more like disappointed. I could relate because I believed that God had let us down, let Dad down and left my mother without the man that took care of her every need.

Mikki kept calling my cell phone, but I simply ignored her calls. She wasn't calling before and now I didn't want to see her at all. For all I knew, she was already kicking it with somebody else and I refused to deal with all of that right now, if ever. We did what we did, and things were different between us anyway. I guess Dad was right when he told us that sex was for marriage and we should wait; perhaps I should have waited to at least see if Mikki and I would still be together after college.

A few of me and Gerald's friends came by that night and we headed down to my father's man cave to chill and watch his big screen TV. My mother came down and brought us some snacks and drinks so we wouldn't be bothered with all of the traffic coming in and out of our house. Why was it that when someone died, people flocked over to the person's house with food, drinks and memories of the person? Never did get the understanding of that.

"G, you okay?" Gerald wanted to know.

"No..."

"I hear you, Bruh. We have never had as many people in our house than we've had in here today. Some of them I can see, but the others? Who are they anyway?"

"That's what I wanted to know. I should go up there and ask Nana Cee to tell them to help themselves to the front door," I joked with a smirk on my face.

"She's not going to do anything like that...she's in my room resting."

"I guess not..."

The night went by slowly, followed by Sunday and our mother's request that we all be in church the way our father would want us to be. Is she serious? I had no intentions of going, but so that I wouldn't upset her, I went along anyway. The last thing I wanted was to hear someone say, "I'm sorry for your loss," one more time. What does that supposed to mean anyway? "God doesn't make mistakes...just know that your father is in a better place?" Riiiiiight...that's why folks testify in church they are blessed to still be in the land of the living, yet when somebody dies, they're in a better place. This must be stuff passed on from generation to generation because it sure does not make any sense to me today.

I did my best to stay out of my mother's way, only assisting when she asked. Otherwise, I was holed up in my room over the days that followed and led up to my father's wake and funeral. Wake on Wednesday evening followed by the funeral on Thursday morning. I just wanted it to all be over so I could try to prepare myself to live without my father for the rest of my life. I knew one thing to be true above all else...I would never be the same again.

Chapter Twenty-One

My doorbell rang constantly over the next several days and I was grateful for my best friend, Lisa, who made sure she was by my side as much as she possibly could be. I knew that Denise was on her way by plane although she really should not be flying so late into her pregnancy. So many people I haven't seen in so long, Gary's family, my family, church family, co-workers...I didn't think our home would be able to accommodate so many people at one time.

Once my father went down to the funeral home, they brought some really nice folding chairs to the house to help seat our visitors and to ask me some questions. The funeral director did not insist that I come into his office because he knew how difficult it could be, so any final selections were made by me from the comfort of my home. My father did the hard part... picking Gary's casket and deciding on the protection the casket would need in the ground, all the things I really could not be bothered with. Cecelia and I actually worked together to pick out Gary's dark blue suit, white shirt, a tie with blue accents along with his undergarments and shoes. My husband's favorite color was blue, so my Dad picked a beautiful blue casket that matched the suit perfectly.

Change Me For My Season

When the funeral director called me Wednesday morning and asked that the family come and view Gary to see if he was to our liking, I declined, but my parents and Gary's mother went and gave their approval. I wasn't ready to see my husband lying in a casket; never thought I would have to so soon in our lives.

With the final plans completed, the wake and funeral set, all I wanted to do was sleep, but I have not once slept in our bed since Gary passed. I waited until everyone left and slept on the sofa in the den. Well, when sleep would fall on me. Trying to make my heart accept what my mind knew was becoming more and more difficult with every passing day. My husband would never come home again.

Going to the wake was a difficult decision for me because I didn't want to go...but I'm the wife, I'm supposed to be there. This is what I told myself as I dressed in a dark blue dress, blue Ferragamo pumps I'd recently purchased from Nordstrom's. Later that evening I regretted wearing a new pair of heels without walking in them at home first.

When we arrived at the church, Gary's mother was on her knees in front of the casket rubbing on him. I could tell by the shaking of her shoulders that she was crying, but no sound escaped her. It wasn't until one of the funeral directors approached and let her know that the rest of the family had arrived and wanted a chance to view Gary's body that she moved to a seat on the front pew.

Gerald held onto me as if I would break, and Gary Jr. held Monét's hand and waited while we stepped up to the casket. I'd never touched a dead body, and decided that I wasn't going to touch Gary because I wanted to remember his touch. Not a cold, hard body that no longer had life. Unlike me, Monét walked up and lay her head on her father's shoulder, and with heavy tears streaming down her face, she kissed Gary's cheek and said, "I'll love you forever, Daddy."

Gary Jr. stayed back, and when Monét was through, he walked to the seats designated for us and sat down with us, putting his shades on to hide his eyes. Normally I would have fussed at him about it, but I felt there was no need this time.

People came in waves, something I'd never seen before.

The church would fill up and then it would empty, only to fill up again over the two hours the wake was held. When it was just about over, one of the ministers from our church expressed his thanks to everyone on behalf of our family and reminded them that the funeral would be held the following morning at 10 a.m., followed by the burial and cemetery, and afterwards the repast at the church. I was relieved when he prayed and dismissed us so we could go to our several homes. I was not receiving any visitors that night because I knew the next day would be the most difficult for our family.

The following day we walked into a packed church, every single seat on the pews were occupied and the chairs added to aisles as well. As our family made the procession to view Gary's body one last time, I heard some crying and plenty of sniffles all wrapped up in a cocoon. I refused to look at anyone for fear I would see the grief I was feeling mirrored in their faces. But it did no good because as soon as I walked up to the casket and knew that it would be the last time I would see his handsome face, my knees became weak and I fell on my husband's chest and cried. I just cried and held onto him, trying to will him back to life somehow. Next thing I knew, a pair of strong arms gently lifted me and helped me to my seat. When I looked up, it was Gary Jr. with his own tears making separate paths down his cheeks. He comforted me and waited until everyone else finished and returned to his father's casket, kissed his forehead, touched his hands and returned to his seat beside me.

I immediately tuned out most of the service because I was simply numb. There were so many nice things said about the man I loved with all that was within me, and I heard some of them. There were those who addressed our family directly, letting us know they were praying for us, and even someone who stated they knew that nothing that was said will bring comfort today, but eventually God will get us through. That's when I heard Gary Jr. say, "Got that right nothing being said is helping," under his breath.

Holding it together to try and display a strength that I did not have was ruined when Nicole, the young teenager that I'd mentored some years back, sang Gary's favorite song: God Is. At first the song had not penetrated the walls I erected around my heart, but when Nicole put her own spin on it, singing about God's healing, deliverance and so on, I completely lost it again. Not because the Lord was touching my heart so good, but because the very song that my husband loved will no longer be sung to him by me. I won't hear him humming the tune while I sing the words and we worship God together in our special way.

Pastor Jackson did a wonderful job eulogizing Gary, so I'm told, but I hardly heard a word. I know he mentioned I was his Goddaughter and Gary was like a son to him, dutiful and faithful to his family, his career and his church. Most of all, he loved everyone and was a great help to the ministry at Redeemed Church of God in Christ. He shared some great times and even had some of the people laughing about my husband, who was a jokester at times himself, but I could not respond to any of it.

The burial was definitely something I didn't want to go to because, as Pastor Jackson said, it is Gary's final resting place. Well, at least his body's final resting place because Gary is no longer with us. Pastor Jackson stood at the head of my husband's casket and I heard him talking, but the words he said didn't mean much to me. It was when he took flowers and allowed the crushed petals to fall on the casket that I completely lost it.

"Foreasmuch as it has pleased Almighty God to take out of this world our deceased brother, we commit his body to Mother Earth, earth to earth, ashes to ashes, dust to dust, looking for the general resurrection in the last day, and the life of the world to come, through our Lord Jesus Christ: at whose second coming in glorious majesty to judge the world, the earth and the sea shall give up their dead; and the corruptible bodies of those who sleep in Him shall be changed, and made like unto His own glorious body, according to the working whereby he is able to subdue all things in Himself. Amen."

How my pastor was able to continue the graveside ceremony having those assembled to repeat the Lord's Prayer after him and conclude by reading Revelations 14:13 and the benediction is beyond me. I cannot explain what came over me, but my sons had me by both of my arms, half carrying/half walking me back to the limo. I heard myself, but I could not control my emotions. Everything that I'd held in over the months of Gary's illness came pouring out of me and I was no longer…me.

My sons sat in the limo on either side of me, both trying to comfort me the best they could, but I could not be consoled; not right away. My mother-in-law sat there quietly, seemingly in her own world, her emotions showing in the form of the tears that trickled down her face. Gary Jr. reached over and pulled his grandmother into his arms and held her like a baby while we all tried to pull ourselves together on the way back to the church for the repast.

Once we arrived, I went to my pastor's office to sit in there alone for a while. I wasn't ready to see and talk to anyone, I just couldn't do it. After about a half hour, I grabbed some tissues from the box on Pastor Jackson's desk and found myself walking into the sanctuary where I last saw my husband's casket. I walked to the altar where it had laid barely an hour before, looked at some of the petals from the flowers that remained on the floor, the only evidence that there had been a funeral. I walked from one end of the altar to the other, trying with all that was within me to accept the fact that when we returned home later today that Gary would not be there.

I had no idea how many times I'd walked that altar, but soon Chad joined me. He didn't say a word at first, just walked with me as I slowly tried to make sense of it all.

"Sis, you need to come on down and grab a bite to eat. You're going to need your strength." Chad encouraged.

"I know, Chad," I looked at him with tear-filled eyes. "I know…it's…hard."

"Aw, Sis, I know it is. No one can describe this pain, but know that we're here for you…I'm here for you."

"Thank you…is Tiana here with you today?"

"She's downstairs waiting on me to come back. I wanted to check on you though."

"I appreciate it. Well," I said, wiping at the tears that refused to stop flowing, "I'd better get down there with my children before they think I abandoned them."

"Come on, it's going to be okay. If you need to get out of here early, just tell me and I'll make sure you get home. That good?"

"It's good," I attempted to smile through my tears.

The fellowship hall was crowded, but it made no difference to me. My plate remained untouched and I spoke to and received hugs and words of encouragement from so many people in the next hour or more that my head pounded with pain. I needed to go home, but I stayed there knowing that I would never go home to or with my husband ever again.

The Transformation

"And be not conformed to this world: but be ye transformed by the renewing of your mind, that ye may prove what is that good, and acceptable, and perfect, will of God." Romans 12:2

Chapter Twenty-Two

TONYA

Indefinite leave of absence is what I requested from the Board of Education. My position would not be held and I could have cared less. Taking showers each morning was a chore that I considered skipping, but I didn't want to find out how long I could go without washing before I couldn't stand myself. Moving in any way was laborious and I did as little as possible. If Monét wasn't at my parents' house, she was with Gary's mother because I just couldn't get it together to do more than wash and change into a clean pair of pajamas each day.

It had only been about three weeks after Gary's passing but the dark cloud that followed me every day didn't appear to be letting up. I wasn't concerned about it at all because there was almost no reason for me to do anything or go anywhere, with the exception of church, and that's because my parents came by and picked me up. I'd gotten very used to not talking much, so when my father asked me when I planned to return to school, Monét told him, "I'm already going back to school, Granddad."

"I'm talking about my 'Baby Girl,' *Baby Girl*," my father smiled at Monét through the rearview mirror.

"Oooooooh, ok Granddad," she answered, putting her ear plugs to her phone in her ears. I never bothered to ask her who bought her cell phone, but I'm sure it was Cecelia Simmons.

"Tonya? What are your plans?" my father addressed me directly. My mother hummed because she knew I was not in much of a mood to talk.

"I don't have any plans, I'm…not ready to go back to work."

Surprisingly my father nodded and started a conversation with my mother and I tuned them out as I prepared to, yet again, listen to more condolences and assurances from the members of my church. I wasn't ungrateful, it just was not going to change my current situation. My husband's body was buried six feet under, his soul has been returned to God and the man I knew no longer occupied the body I was accustomed to snuggling with every night. So I smiled and thanked everyone; no further conversation was necessary. The '*I'm so sorry, Tonya,*' or '*Things will be better before you know it, just give it time,*' and oh, the one I hated the most: "*God doesn't make mistakes; your husband is in a better place.*" Nothing that was said helped me… nothing.

My mother wanted me to come and have dinner at her house because my sons would be there along with Monét, but all I wanted was to go home and crawl into my bed. It took a week for me to actually sleep in my room on the sheets that Gary last laid upon. I wanted to smell him every day, so I took the sheets off of the bed, folded them and placed them in a very large plastic bag that zipped closed. The bag has a permanent place under my husband's pillow, and I take a moment each night to open it slightly to smell his scent and the cologne he loved to wear. This way, I knew that a part of him would be with me for as long as possible.

"Tonya, just for a little while, okay? You need a good meal; I know you're not eating like you should," my mother urged, side-eyeing me.

I acquiesced. Why bother to argue when talking wasn't on my list of priorities. The visit wasn't long, but I further pleased my mother by eating a small amount of everything she cooked, wrapped an additional plate and asked my father to miss part of a basketball game to take me home. He was none too happy about it, but one look at my sad face convinced him that maybe I really needed to go home. I knew I could have gotten one of my guys to take me, but my father was funny about letting anyone drive his car.

No sooner had I walked through the front door, my house phone started ringing. Ignoring it, I headed up to my bedroom to remove my clothes and put on a comfortable pair of pajamas with plans to head down to the den and relax for the rest of the day. Still the phone continued to ring. Whoever was calling me refused to leave a message, just continued to call back-to-back until I finally answered.

"Tonya!" Lisa screamed in my ear.

"What? What's wrong and why in the world are you ringing my phone like that?" I asked with my heart racing.

"Ton, I tried to catch you before you left your parents' house, but Denise had to be rushed to the hospital! You've got to meet me there..."

"Wait, I thought Denise went back home?"

"She was supposed to, but her father wasn't feeling too well, so she extended her time here..."

"Why didn't anybody tell me that?" I wanted to know, cutting Lisa off.

"That's neither here nor there right now, she's headed to the hospital and I believe she was hemorrhaging," Lisa explained.

"Uh, are you on your way?"

"I am now, do you want me to swing by and pick you up?'

"No, I'm not up for going to the hospital, but keep me posted."

"Tonya? Denise needs us and you..."

"And I what, Lisa? Do you realize just three weeks ago I was in that hospital with my husband watching him...die?" I sobbed on the last word.

"Ton, I'm sorry, I wasn't thinking. Listen, I'll keep you posted, just please pray for our friend. Can you do that?"

"Yes, I'll do that," I sniffled. "Please...keep me posted."

After hanging up with Lisa, I called my Mom to tell her about Denise and she prayed while I listened. We ended the prayer and I found a program to watch on TV while I ignored the nudge in my heart to pray for Denise and her baby. There was a part of me that did not believe my prayers would make much difference, and since my mother prayed, that should suffice…but I knew better. The harder I tried to push Denise out of my mind, the stronger the urge to kneel and pray until I finally gave in and prayed for my friend. It is the first time in months that I'd prayed for someone so fervently besides Gary, but it blessed me too.

Once my prayer ended, I made sure the doors were all locked and headed to bed to sniff my husband's scent and try to find sleep amidst my tears and memories.

~~~~~~~~~

Denise gave birth to a baby girl that weighed just under five pounds. She was perhaps a few weeks early, but the baby wasn't doing well at all. Lisa told me, "Girl, that poor baby has tubes running here, there and everywhere, not to mention she's having difficulty breathing. I told Denise her butt was too old to be trying to have a baby."

Since the first night I prayed for Denise, I prayed for her and the baby constantly. I would remind myself that Denise was going to put her up for adoption, but from what I understand, she's been at the hospital as much as possible since she was released.

Monét was upstairs in her room with Dana, and I was in the kitchen preparing a light snack since Lisa, along with her children, would be stopping by. We had not laid eyes on each since Gary's funeral, but I was looking forward to spending time with my best friend and catching up on things in her life.

Dawn is a year older than Monét and Dana, but she seemed to fit right into friendships with my daughter and her friends. Having always been a happy child, it was some getting used to seeing Dawn not smile as much. Her parents' divorce was weighing pretty heavy on her, and I'm sure Lisa has not bothered to begin fixing things amicably for the sake of Dawn and BJ.

When the doorbell rang, I felt an unexpected surge of excitement course through my body just knowing Lisa was on the other side of the door. Before I could get there, Monét was answering the door.

"Hey Auntie Lisa! Hey Dawn…where's BJ? I thought he was coming too."

"My brother said he doesn't want to spend the day around a bunch of girls, so he's hanging with my granddad," Dawn explained while fixing her long hair into a ponytail. She is the spitting image of her mother without the attitude and the propensity to fight at the drop of a hat when we were her age.

I welcomed my friend with a hug and invited her in so we could catch up on all I'd missed over the last few months. I didn't see or talk to Lisa very much when Gary was sick either, so I was looking forward to a long visit with my best friend.

"What are you doing with the living room? I like the swatches of blues and beiges I see you working with," Lisa told me as she took a seat on the sofa in the den.

"I haven't changed it in so long…it's just time, you know?" I started it, but stopped because I no longer had my husband to approve of my ideas.

"If you need some help, just let me know. Otherwise, how are you? Honestly?"

"You're the first person I actually took the time to sit down and visit with other than going to my parents' house…honestly, it's been hard…very hard. For the most part Monét isn't even here and I feel guilty, but I can't pull myself together enough to hear her share her day most times, but I'm purposely trying to get better."

"Girl, listen, you've got to allow yourself to get better… admit how you're feeling and then deal with it. I know you're saved and trust God and all of that, but you're human too. It's a process…"

"How do you know, Lisa? Granted you're dealing with a loss but it's not the same!"

"Take it down, girly, I'm just trying to help my best friend out. No, I haven't been through such a great loss, but with anything, there is always a process. My divorce is a loss, and believe it or not, your advice on how to deal with it concerning my children is something I decided to try…and you know what? It turns out that you were right," Lisa pushed my shoulder with hers. "You helped me, so let me help you the best I know how. Please?"

"Okay, Lisa," I gave in, letting the tears I held go free.

Lisa pulled me into a hug and let me cry for as long as I needed to, which felt like an eternity. By the time I was able to get my tears under control, my eyes were puffy and red, and my nose was stuffed up.

When I finally got it together, Lisa and I changed the subject about serious things and discussed how I planned to move forward with redecorating the living room. Of course she wanted to help me, but she had no clue that I was going to let her do the entire room. I just wanted a change so that everything didn't look like Gary still lived in the house, and yet I wanted nothing to be different in an attempt to keep things as they were at the same time.

Out of the blue, Lisa asked, "Have you tried to call Denise?"

When I looked at Lisa, she was fiddling with the swatches and never looked at me. Lisa knew good and well I haven't called Denise. What was I supposed to say to someone when it's a possibility that they may lose a loved one when I don't know what's appropriate for someone to say to me when I lost Gary.

"No...I mean, how would I know the right time to reach her? Isn't the baby in the N.I.C.U.?" I skirted around the real issue.

"Keep telling yourself that's a good enough excuse to not at least try to reach her if that makes you feel good, but you and I both know better than that."

"What did she name the baby? I never did ask..."

"You don't even know that?" Lisa asked, shaking her head. "I needed you with me to help me talk her out of naming her '*myangel.*' Really? Denise knows that wasn't going to fly with me, some old ghetto sounding name. I told her to think it over and get back to me."

"You have got to be kidding me! Well, what did she finally name her?" I wanted to know.

"Shouldn't tell you, but since I brought it up, I will. She named her Nia Solange..."

"Beautiful! Now that makes better sense than some '*myan-gel*,' just wait until I see that crazy girl."

"And when will that be? When the baby is four or five months old?'

"I will, Lisa, I will...did she say why she chose those names?"

"Simple...the baby was born on purpose for a purpose so it's Nia, and because she's her angel, Solange actually means 'angel," Lisa explained while she continued to play with the swatches of fabric.

As bad as I wanted to go and see Denise's little angel, going back to that hospital is something I vowed I'd never do when I left the morning of my husband's passing. There is no way I could see changing my mind any time soon, but I purposed to call Denise to let her know that both she and the baby are constantly in my prayers. They're the only ones I've been praying for lately.

To ease the guilt I felt, after Lisa and Dawn left, I called Denise's phone and left her a message letting her know that I have been praying for her and baby Nia, and for her to call me if she needed me. Not even five minutes later, the doorbell rang. When I looked through the peephole, there Denise stood. I opened the door and opened my arms to a sobbing Denise, her pain penetrating my being and my heart feeling her sorrow. She had finally received what she needed from me, and that is to know I cared. A simple phone call.

Chapter Twenty-Three

GARY JR.

I'm in trouble...*big* trouble. Nothing I planned to do purposely, but here it is...here I am. My thoughts after the semester ended was to go home and chill for the summer, stay in shape for football and hang with my friends. But no, I get a call from Mikki saying she *thinks* she's pregnant. All the stuff they sell in the drugstore and a free clinic in the city, and this girl is telling me she thinks she's pregnant? I couldn't tell Moms because she's just starting to get back to being herself and I sure didn't need to tell her something that would pull her back into her self-imposed hiatus from life. But who could I talk to about this?

"Aaaaaah, Nana Cee would tell me what to do," I loudly proclaimed. I had the coolest grandmother in the world, and nothing knocked her off her axis unless she wanted it to. Putting in a call to her resulted in her inviting me and Mikki over the next day for lunch.

Waiting a whole 24 hours to talk to my grandmother made me antsy. Mikki thought it was a coincidence that I asked her to roll with me to my grandmother's house, but I couldn't take any chances of her deciding not to go. When we arrived, my grandmother had a healthy lunch already waiting for us and some conversation too. It wasn't until Mikki alluded to the fact that she might be pregnant that Nana Cee took the reins and rolled forward...hard.

"Are you trying to tell me that you might be pregnant by my grandson?"

"Well, yes...I'm late," Mikki told Nana Cee while she pushed her vegetables around her plate.

"Have you seen a doctor, taken a pregnancy test?"

"I took one a couple weeks ago, but it was negative...and I'm still late."

"Did you take the test right? 'Cause I have one that you can use right now..."

"No, that's okay," Mikki was quick to say with her eyes wide. "I'm just going to go to the doctor."

"Gary, Baby, come here a minute," Nana Cee ordered as she got up from the table. She didn't look back, so that meant I was to follow right behind her.

As soon as we reached her bedroom, she closed the door behind us.

"When was the last time you slept with that girl?"

"It was before my Dad..."

"Okay, so nothing happened between you two during that period of time."

"Not since winter break, just before I went back to school."

"This girl is saying she's late now...has she told you how far along she thinks she might be? I know every pregnancy is different, but I can assure you, Miss Mikki ain't no more pregnant than I am, and I can't imagine a pregnancy."

"How do you know this, Nana Cee? I mean, I did sleep with her and it's a possibility that she's pregnant by me..."

"Did you use protection?"

"Always, but that doesn't mean anything..."

"And it's May on my calendar. Baby, let me tell you something about women...we have a mental calendar for everything. You may not see it written down, and we may give the impression that we're not keeping up with things...but trust me, we are. Now this little, I don't know what to call her, is trying to set you up. Not that she's pregnant now, so that she can get pregnant by you going forward. She wants you to commit to her in a way you're not in any way, shape or form to do. Now," Nana Cee continued as she opened a drawer and pulled out a bag to hand to me, "You take this with you and insist the little heifer take the test at your house. Go in the basement if you have to, and make sure she follows the directions. Shoot, a fool can't err the instructions are so simple! I guarantee you, she ain't pregnant...and tell her that I said her period is due in a day or two because I smell her."

"You smell her? Mikki doesn't stink, Nana Cee," I defended.

"I didn't say she stinks, Gary Simmons, Jr.; there is a smell that comes when a woman is about to have her monthly...as long as the body is clean, it won't stink, but I've got a good nose and I mean what I said. Go on and take that little sneaky thing out of my house, make me sick trying to set my grandbaby up! She don't know, do she?" my grandmother fussed all the way back to the kitchen.

Before I confronted Mikki two days later about taking the pregnancy test my grandmother gave me, I had to really think about all she told me about women. The only example of relationships I had were my parents and my mother's parents, so to even consider that somebody would try to play me out cut my pride deep. Mikki and I grew up together, so why would she do this to me?

When I could no longer wait to find out if I was going to be a father or not, I invited Mikki over and we went to my father's office in the basement. The first thing I remembered was when my father walked in on us about to get it in for the first time, and how he let me off the hook. That won't be happening now, that's for sure.

"Are you going to take the test or not? I need to know what to tell my Moms, and you know she's not going to be happy about all this."

"I shouldn't, Gary...I mean, I know your mother's still going through your father's death and all, but maybe a baby will make things better."

"How in the…you know what, Michaela, just take the test so we will know how to go forward. Can you do that?"

Mikki snatched the test from my hand and went into the bathroom. When I heard the toilet flush, I walked in without knocking so I could catch her if she was trying to pull a fast one. Surprisingly, Mikki didn't say anything about me walking in on her; we both stood and watched for the color to change on the test. When nothing happened after five minutes, I knew Nana Cee was right.

"You tried to play me…"

"No, I didn't! I'm late and…"

"And we didn't sleep together when I saw you last, so if you're pregnant, it's not mine. You just went and gave what belongs to me to somebody else!"

"Belong to you? This is my body, thank you! I didn't sleep with anyone else…you know what, I'm going home."

"Run, go ahead, but the truth is…"

"The truth is, I'm in love with the only guy I've ever been with my whole life," Mikki stood flat-footed and looked me in my eyes. "Obviously I was wrong in thinking he still loves me."

I grabbed Mikki and pulled her to me, ran my hands down both sides of her body so I could feel the familiar curves that I was afraid someone else might have felt in my absence. Then I kissed her, tasting her spearmint gum, and taking other liberties with my hands as I explored her body. When Mikki started unbuttoning my shirt, all I could think of was joining my body with hers again.

Pushing Mikki towards the sofa in the office, I pulled her shirt over her head and unsnapped her bra behind her back. She unfastened my pants and I let them drop to the floor, followed by me snatching her shorts and underwear down to her ankles all at once. Just as I was about to cover Mikki's body with mine…

"Gary! What are…Mikki? Oh no, this is *not* going on under my roof! You're just going to disrespect me, this house? You have lost your mind! I want you out of my house, right now…you're no longer welcome here, Michaela," my mother said before the tears fell from her eyes and she quickly turned and ran back up the basement steps.

Mikki sat on the sofa with both hands covering her breasts with her head down, embarrassment and sadness played across her face.

"I'm sorry…"

Mikki held up one of her hands to halt my words. I guess there really was nothing left to say. She silently dressed and asked me to let her out the basement door; I couldn't blame her. The hard part was going upstairs to talk to my mother, and as soon as my foot hit the top step in the kitchen, my mother jumped down my throat.

"You think you're such the grown man now, huh? You're so grown that you feel like you don't have to respect my house, that's what you think!"

"Mom, no, it just happened, I didn't plan it…"

"You didn't plan it, is that your excuse? In your father's office, Gary?" my mother cried, her sobs grew louder and louder.

I reached out to hug my mother, but she pulled away from me, something she'd never done to me her whole life. I looked at the woman who had to have lost close to forty pounds since my father died, her clothes literally sagging on her slight frame. The light that once danced in her eyes, the love that was always evident for me was gone, and her body shook with the hurt I caused.

"Mom…I'm sorry, I didn't mean to disrespect you in any way. Please, Mom, can I explain to you…"

"Why you and your girlfriend felt it was okay to get naked and have sex in my house? Absolutely not!" she said, walking hard towards the den with me on her heels.

"Can I at least explain? I wasn't trying to hurt you…"

"No explanation is needed, I don't want to see Mikki in this house again, do you hear? And understand something…I'm not blaming her, I'm blaming you!" my mother screamed at me just as the doorbell rang. Neither of us moved, but I saw Gerald headed for the door in my peripheral view.

"You can blame me, Mom; as a grown man, I take responsibility for my actions, I just want to explain to you what happened."

"Don't want to hear it," my mother told me, not bothering to look at me.

"So you don't want to hear what I have to say, yet you're telling me that I'm being disrespectful?" Now I was starting to get angry with my mother although I couldn't understand why.

"That's exactly what I said! Get out of my presence before I say something to you I might feel bad about later, because trust me when I tell you, I will," my mother said with clenched teeth.

Her anger made me even angrier and I said, "Whatever! But it's alright for *Uncle Chad* to be up in *this house* every week."

When I turned to head up to my room, a big fist grabbed me up in the collar of my shirt and immediately the bottom of that same fist thumped me in the middle of my chest...*painful!*

"If I ever hear you, or hear talk of you speaking to your mother in a disrespectful manner ever again, I will knock your head smooth off. You hear me?" my grandfather asked me with a sneer on his face I'd never seen before. Obviously I didn't answer fast enough because he asked again, "Do you *hear* me?"

"Ye-yes, Granddad, I hear you," was my stammered answer. I didn't know he had that much strength in him.

"Your father was the man of this house and he didn't leave anyone else as the head in his absence. God is the head of *this* house, and don't you forget it," my grandfather dismissed me.

As soon as I reached the top of the steps, the doorbell rang again, and I heard Gerald greeting Uncle Chad. I know he's feeling my Moms now that my father is gone and he's a married man. Yet I'm disrespecting this house? We'll see about that.

Chapter Twenty-Four

TONYA

Six months. For the first time in quite some time, it feels like time is standing still. Six whole months my husband has been gone, and I still cannot get myself together. I've learned to put on a good front for everyone else, but no one sees my tears every night when I slightly open the plastic bag under Gary's pillow so I can smell his scent...and cry. I miss my husband so much, and my heart hurts so badly that my chest is sore. There are days I still do not descend the steps, and my daughter probably thinks I've checked out as her mother. I know I have to do better, but it's been much easier to think it than to do it.

My shower was finished and I'd just put on a fresh night gown so I could climb back under the covers when my bedroom door flew open and the last person I expected to see came through it...Cecelia Simmons.

"Good morning, Tonya," she spoke in my direction as she proceeded to the curtains and blinds and opened them wide.

"What in the world are you doing?" I squinted to get a better look at my mother-in-law. "I don't want any light in here."

"You don't have a choice but to let the light in, in more ways than one. Monét needs to be fitted for some new bras, school is in a few weeks and she needs clothes too. Who better to take her to do that than her mother? Let's go, get up, chop-chop!"

Cecelia was just too over the top cheery for me at nine o'clock in the morning. My response was to pull the cover over my head and turn my back. I was not getting up to shop anywhere. She could take Monét and spend the whole day in the mall like they usually do. I'm not in the mood.

When I felt the breeze of the cover lift over me and both feet being pulled to the bottom of the bed, I was shocked.

"Cecelia, seriously? I'm not going anywhere today."

"You haven't been anywhere in months. Time to rejoin the rest of the living and today is as good a day to start," Cecelia expressed, sitting next to me on the bed. "Tonya, I know how hard it is…Gary is my only son, and the pain of losing him is the worst I've ever experienced in my life. He came from me! But you know what? He wouldn't want us sitting around here moping and taking a break from living when he lived his life to the fullest. He was a good man, he loved his family and he took care of us…all of us. Time to check back in, Baby. Your children need you…we all need you."

Tears seeped through my closed eyelids as I let my mother-in-laws words flow through me and register in my head and touch my heart. I knew she was right, but how? How could I live like I've always lived when my heart was gone forever?

"Let's go, Tonya, we have some shopping to do," my mother-in-law pulled on me again. "Go on and hit the shower…"

"I've already showered, but I'll go wash my face and brush my teeth again. Give me about 15 minutes and I'll be downstairs."

When I went into the bathroom, I decided not to avoid the woman I saw in the mirror. My face was gaunt and my shoulder bones were showing through my skin. I had bags under my eyes so heavy I didn't think the foundation would hide it today. Dull skin and dead looking eyes completed my look, but I decided I would put on a good face for my daughter today. She deserves better than I've been giving her.

Returning to my room, I noticed the linen was removed from my bed and the plastic bag was gone from under Gary's

172

pillow.

"Cecelia! Cecelia!" I ran to my open bedroom door. "What are you doing to my bed? Bring everything back in here...*now!*"

"What is all the screaming about? I figured I'd help you out..."

"Where's the plastic bag?"

"It's in your bedroom. I didn't know what it was, so I didn't bother opening it."

Sighing, I grabbed the clean linen from my mother-in-law's hands and threw them on my unmade bed. "I changed everything yesterday, thank you. Next time just ask me."

"Okay, I'm sorry," she responded with her hands held up in surrender. "Why don't I see if you have something cute to wear in here."

"I can choose my own clothing..."

"Why do you still have Gary's clothing in here? You haven't gotten rid of anything, have you?"

"Can I have some privacy to get dressed please? Gary's things aren't going anywhere right now...I'll deal with it... whenever," I waved my hand dismissing the subject.

"You won't push his memory away if you give his things away...he's always with you. But I'm going downstairs with Miss Mo, so when you're ready," Cecelia told me when she saw the squint in my eyes. I felt like throwing her down the stairs!

Donning a pair of shades to help hide the bags that make up wouldn't and I found a dress that I couldn't get into for years, I joined my daughter and my mother-in-law for a shopping trip that was not on my list of things to do for the day. Monét kept herself busy in the back texting on her phone, and Cecelia kept my attention by talking about any and everything all the way to the mall.

Our first stop was the lingerie shop so Monét can get measured for new bras. She told me a couple months back that she was peeking out on the sides, but I thought she might have been exaggerating until I saw how ill-fitting her bra was when she took off her t-shirt.

"Yes, she got those double-d's from her Nana Cee," Cecelia

smiled. "But we have to make sure her cleavage doesn't stick out like that anymore and good support is key for the back."

We watched while the sales lady measured my daughter and I couldn't stop my mind from drifting back to a conversation I tried to have with Gary last year concerning Monét and how quickly she was developing.

"Baby Girl is getting tall," Gary stated after Monét left out of our bedroom asking if we would buy her a cell phone.

"Speaking of," I said as I got out of bed, "I'm going to have to get your daughter fitted for a bra."

"Fitted? Why can't you do like you've been doing and go in the teen department and get her some new ones? I don't see the problem." Gary said, sitting up on the side of the bed.

"Tell me you haven't seen how much Monét's body is maturing. If I didn't know I had her, I would have believed she was your mother's daughter since she looks just like her and is built like her too. All those boobs and butt, and her waist is going to be tiny just like Cecelia Simmons too. By the time she turns 16, you're going to start looking into buying a gun, I'm telling you."

"Not Baby Girl, she's fine..."

"In your "Daddy's Baby Girl" eyes she's fine. The way she's sprouting, it won't be long before she..."

"I don't want to hear it!" Gary interrupted me. "I'm not trying to see my daughter as a woman until she becomes one. Stop rushing it."

"Wooo okay, I won't say anything else, I'll just handle it," I told my delusional husband, throwing a pillow at him.

"Mom? Can I get this lacy bra? Mom? *Mom!*"

"What? What did you say?"

"The question is, where did you go," Cecelia side-eyed me. "We're trying to help pick the bras Monét wants so the order can be placed."

"Oh...not the one with all of that lace, it's too grown. You can have the ones with a little lace, and some solids...black, nude, white..."

"Why can't I have the all lacy one? Dana has push-ups and all kinds of…"

"Oh, we are not going to get into what Dana's mother allows her to have today. You will get what I said, that's it and that's all. Unless you want to keep wearing the ones that are too small, close your mouth," I allowed my frustration to play out with Monét. "Say 'but Mom' one time, and this whole shopping trip is over."

When Monét started to cross her arms, Cecelia pulled her aside and had a few words with her. Within seconds her face was straightened and an apology left her lips. Quite honestly, I wanted her to push just a little more because I wanted to go home…shopping was hardly on my priority list.

The rest of the shopping trip went well, and Monét's improved attitude helped. We shopped the rest of the morning and into the afternoon, finally deciding to go to the food court. I couldn't help but think about the times my friends and I frequented the mall and ended up at the same food court checking for guys and having fun. Our teenage years were spent right here, thinking we were so grown and knew it all. Denise's first boyfriend, the newest clothes we could buy within our allowances, the record store and the food court. I had to smile at the memory of it all and be thankful for the friendships that were still intact between us, wishing crazy Sasha was still here.

Our shopping spree ended at a baby boutique where I purchased baby clothing for little Nia Solange, who would be released from the hospital in about another week. She was a beautiful baby who had struggled for so long to live that there were many times I thought I would have to find another black dress. The baby would simply stop breathing because the doctors and nurses said she would just forget and Denise would lose it every single time. But Nia is a little fighter with her bright light brown eyes and caramel colored skin looking nothing like Denise. It didn't matter because my friend made several decisions while she waited for her little girl to get well.

The night I'd called Denise and she ended up on my doorstep was a welcomed surprise. We both tried to figure out why we didn't connect during such a difficult time, and until we spoke to each other, speculation played a negative part in it. Denise thought I was mad at her for something she'd done while carrying the baby, and I thought she only wanted Lisa to be there for her. How wrong we both were.

After Denise and I both calmed down, we had a long talk about what the baby was going through, what I was going through and concluded that we needed each other just like we always had all these years. However, I was not prepared for the bombshell Denise dropped on me when she told me that her baby was sick because she really didn't take care of herself during the pregnancy. Upset because the father decided that he was only going to be a sperm donor and drop a check in the mail, Denise didn't want the baby. Not wanting to feel guilty about aborting, she just ate all kinds of junk, didn't take her prenatal vitamins and did nothing to nourish herself. When Nia was born with so much wrong with her and needing two surgeries during the whole ordeal, the guilt was worse than it was when she aborted her first baby.

"I thought Lisa had told you and you were being…you… and judging me based on the foolish things I'd done," Denise ashamedly explained.

"Lisa hasn't mentioned anything to me about what happened or the reason the baby is sick. Judge you? Why would I do that?"

"You know, Tonya, you have let me know how you felt in years past and I thought this was no different, but this time you wrote me off."

"I didn't come to the hospital because it hasn't been that long since my husband died, and I vowed I would never return. I'm sure it sounds selfish to you, but I just cannot go back into that hospital, any hospital."

"Believe it or not, I understand, I do. You have no idea how glad I am that you're not mad at me."

"Girl, please! Listen, I understand how you feel to some degree. I'm sure you felt like your life was repeating itself all over again, and your heart couldn't take that rejection. You didn't make a good decision, but little Nia is going to be fine.

I'm praying, my family is praying and my mother put her name on the prayer list at our church. She has no choice but to make it," I encouraged Denise.

"But Tonya..."

"I know, Gary didn't make it and all of those same people were praying for him too. I've thought about that before I ever prayed for you and the baby. I was compelled to pray and have been praying ever since. Can't explain it, but I know everything is going to be all right," I smiled.

Denise further explained that she had fibroids and they had started syphoning blood from the baby and she figured whatever happened would happen until she gave birth to the prettiest little girl she had ever seen. This only added to the baby's health problems once she was born and Denise could not shake the guilt until things began turning around.

We talked for quite some time, reminisced and promised each other we would do our best to have each other's backs. I wanted Denise to stay over, but she wanted to get home to her father who was just getting to the place that he was feeling better. He retired and seemed to go downhill quickly because he never did anything but go to work and home to sit in front of the TV in his big, lumpy chair. I guess some things never change.

Chapter Twenty-Five

GARY JR.

I don't know about Gerald, but I was ready to get back on campus and far away from Michaela and the strained relationship with my mother. We never talked about the incident with Mikki again, but it took some time before my mother would accept my hugs again. Man that really hurt. As bad as I wanted to tell Moms, I thought it best that I didn't do anything to make her angry all over again. She's finally spending more time out of her bedroom than she used to, but if I could get her to eat better I'd probably feel better.

My grandfather had helped my brother and I purchase pre-owned vehicles over the summer, both of us choosing Hondas. I wanted a 2010 Honda Civic coupe, dark red, five-speed, fully loaded. Granddad had to teach me how to drive a stick, but I caught on quickly so I could hit the road with no mishaps.

Gerald's 2010 Honda Accord is silver, fully loaded and a four-door. When I asked him why he needed all that room, he said, "You never know what the future may hold." He's been seeing a young lady he met at our Jurisdictional Convocation this summer, so his time was occupied the last two weeks or so with dates and phone calls. Cool! My brother has finally met someone that he can get serious with. Dad would be proud of him. I know I am.

With so much going on in my head, the afternoon I finished getting things together for school, I returned home to find Uncle Chad's police cruiser in front of our house...again. Dude has no idea how badly I wanted to tell him to stay away from my mother. I don't care how long they've known each other, grew up together or whatever, it's time for me to let him know that he should keep driving past this house.

When I opened the door, I could hear my mother laughing and talking, something she doesn't do a lot since Dad died. But here she was, laughing it up with Uncle Chad like everything was cool. I started to walk by the den and head up to my room without saying a word, but my mother would have had my head.

"Hey, Mom...Uncle Chad..."

"Gary Jr., how're you doing son?"

"Son? Are you serious?"

"Gary, what's wrong with you? Chad has been welcome in this house..."

"Don't you think he's visiting a lot more since Dad..." I always say in my mind that my father died, but I don't like saying it out loud.

"Gary, what you don't know is that your father asked me before he passed away to come and check on you all. He called me a week or so before he was last in the hospital, showed me how he set things up for you and asked me to be here...I hope that's not a problem," Chad told me. Right...my father couldn't get my grandfather to do it?

"Yeah, okay, if you say so. Mom, I'm going to finish packing for school."

End of discussion, don't say anything else to me about my father, take care of your own family, and leave the care of our family to our family. These thoughts ran through my mind as I headed up to my room. I was heated! Dad could have told Gerald and I that he asked his best friend to keep an eye on us... we would have reminded him that we got this.

I'd been gathering my things and packing clothes for about an hour when there was a knock on the door. I knew it wasn't Gerald because he would have walked in as he knocked. Wasn't

Moms either, so I didn't answer until the second knock.

"It's open…"

"Hey, listen, Gary…I don't mean to cause any ill feelings between you and me. I've been a part of the Henderson family probably before I knew who I was and I'm going to honor my friendship with your father by carrying out his last wishes. So here, take this letter he wrote you. Your dad was very wise and he knew his children very well. He told me when things got to this point to give you this letter because it would be time for you to receive what he has to say to you," Chad explained.

I could see his sincerity, but I didn't acknowledge it. I took the letter and dismissed him by not commenting on anything he said. Hint was received because once I turned my back, I heard my bedroom door close quietly.

My hands shook with fear, anticipation and excitement as I carefully opened the envelope with my name on it written by my father. The first genuine smile crossed my face since before my father's illness.

Dear Gary Jr.

I know where your head is, so I've got to share some things with you that you're going to need as you continue to advance in adulthood. Did you know that our name means, "brave warrior?" That is you, my namesake; that is you.

I read some more but could hardly see it because of the tears that kept getting in the way. Finally, he ended the letter:

Son, I love you more than I could ever put into words in a letter or tell you out of my mouth. You are my firstborn and a lot of responsibility is assumed to be assigned to you, but I want you and Gerald to work it out like you always do. Keep an eye on your mother and your sister for me. I don't want your sister to seek out an unhealthy relationship because she's missing something with me. I pray that I've loved each of you enough that you have everything you need. To make sure that you're covered in every area, trust God with full abandon. He loves you more than I.

Love,

Your father for life and beyond

Slowly I folded the letter and put it back in the envelope before I buried my head in my pillow to yell so no one could hear me. *Dad, I need you now!*

Chapter Twenty-Six

TONYA

By the time school started, my sons were back on campus and I was still at home. Sitting under a cloud of depression was getting old, but I could only manage to pull myself from under it so that I can interact with my family and friends. At least I was doing better with my daughter after my mother-in-law insisted I accompany them on a shopping spree to get Monét ready for school. Truth be told, I needed that time away from home to involve myself in something else other than thinking about Gary and the fact that I will never see him again this side of heaven. Oh, Lord, I miss that man! My mornings began with thanking God for another day and a sniff of my husband in that large plastic bag.

I made it clear that I would not be returning to teach full time, but I made myself available to substitute teach, which I figured would be a good change of pace. My husband left us financially secure, so there was no true need for me to worry about working to bring in enough money to sustain the household. Knowing this brought some level of comfort, but not what I would feel if Gary was still here with us.

My parents were worried about me and suggested that I get counseling, but I told them I work on myself every day...

between the tears anyway. The one word question I have daily is 'why?' Why my husband, my children's father, when he was one of the nicest men you would ever meet. He was committed to his God, his wife, his children, his career…and he loved people. Gary had a heart for hurting men because he knew what it meant to be one. Coming to terms with not growing up with his father and then losing him so early in life messed with his head for a while, but God blessed him to come through it. Especially that pride problem he had early in our marriage. I thought that along with my stubbornness would be the death of our family, but the Lord stepped in and helped us work it out. So then, why did my husband's healing have to take him to the grave?

I pondered these and many other thoughts every day, and sometimes my memories make me smile and even laugh aloud, but those same remembrances cause me so much sadness because I could no longer make new ones with the only man I have ever loved my whole life. Gary loved me just as much as I loved him; we loved on each other too. So much and so until he felt it necessary to write me a letter shortly before he passed. There are days it helps me and days I cry my eyes out yearning to feel his arms around me, loving me in the physical. I love me some him so badly that it hurts as much as it hurts to feel the void of his absence.

Thanksgiving was a ways away, but I was already dreading the holiday. Father's Day around the Simmons household was extra quiet. My sons went their separate ways to deal with it, and Monét chose to sit with me and look at family photos and talk about her father. It was her outlet and way of dealing with her feelings, so I let her for as long as necessary. Holidays are no longer enjoyable for us.

On a day that I felt I would fall into the abyss and stay there forever, my father called to check on me. I have to admit that for the most part, he has left me to myself when it came to dealing with Gary's passing, but I knew sooner or later he would confront me. I put on my fake cheery voice when I saw his cell number and name come up on the TV.

"Hey, Dad, what's going on?"

"Not much, but I was calling to let you know I was stopping by on my way back from the barber...you busy?"

"Um, no, you can come on."

As soon as we hung up, I ran upstairs quickly to find something to put on and make it back downstairs to the ringing of the doorbell in record time. I greeted my father, offered him a seat, a drink and something to eat. He accepted the seat and refused everything else.

"Baby Girl, how're you doing?"

"I'm good..." I answered to my father's head shaking in the negative.

"I'm your Daddy, been knowing you since you were in the womb...I know better. Listen to me and then I'm going home to take you momma to the store. You refused counseling from Pastor Jackson or professionally and things are falling apart. You've semi-checked out and it's time that you come on back... you ain't going nowhere until it's your time no way, so...

"Nevertheless, I'm going to tell you what I was impressed in my spirit to tell you, and that is this; your husband's passing was the best healing anyone could ask for. Why God decided to call him home so soon we may never know. But Gary's the one with the victory. Now, I can't say that I know what it feels like to lose my spouse, but I'm sure yours wouldn't want you moping around pretending to live and allow your family life and ministry to fall by the wayside. Your children still need you, I don't care that Gary Jr. and Gerald are grown men; they will never be too grown not to need you...if they were to take their lead from you, this whole house would be covered in gloom and depression. Pray Baby, Girl, you've got to pray and ask God to help you through this because in spite of how bad you're feeling right now, it's going to get better.

"Stop denying how you feel, tell God and let Him handle it. Oh...that was more than one thing, wasn't it," Dad chuckled lightly. "I love you, you hear me, and you're going to make it... you will always have Gary with you, so help his legacy continue. Think you can do that?

"Last thing, I promise...I'm not telling you how long to grieve, I'd never do that...take all the time you need, but actively involve yourself in the process," my father smiled warmly.

I simply nodded around the lump in my throat as I fought to keep my tears at bay. Once I kissed my Dad's cheek at the door and closed it, I slumped to the floor at the door, unable to take another step. When my father's car pulled away from the curb, I screamed at the top of my lungs until I had no voice left, "God help me, God help me, God help me, God help me, God help me!!!!" If He doesn't, I cannot be helped.

When there was truly nothing left, I literally crawled back to the den, curled up on the sofa and fell into a deep sleep and I dreamed about my husband. He was so beautiful and so happy! His smile penetrated my soul and his joy radiated all through me and he said, "All is well." I kept trying to grab at Gary to pull him to me, but he began backing away with that smile on his face until he faded away.

"Mom? Mommy!" Monét yelled in my face and I jumped awake with a start.

"What…what is it?" I asked barely above a whisper.

"I'm home," my daughter smiled and kissed my cheek. "Do you need some water?"

I motioned that I'd lost my voice and she went on her way as if it were a normal occurrence. Forced to lie back down, my mind was assaulted with the dream I'd had about Gary and how happy he was. Not happy to be without me, but filled with a joy that I could feel and yet could not touch now that I was awake.

With a heavy sigh, I made my way to the kitchen to begin putting a light dinner together for Monét and myself. My appetite was returning and I'd gained back 20 of the 40 pounds I'd lost, to my mother's delight.

"Can't we just order pizza tonight? You won't have to cook," Monét bargained with me.

"No, you are not eating pizza every week; a healthy meal is what we're having tonight."

Nose turned up and teen attitude on the horizon, my daughter had the nerve to say under her breath, "It's not like you're going to eat what you cook anyway…"

Before I knew anything, I'd snatched Monét up and we were eyeball to eyeball.

"Little girl, whatever your problem is, you'd better correct it before I do. You got me?" my voice was hoarse, but I know my daughter heard every single word I'd said. Actually, I surprised myself at how quickly I reacted to her sassy mouth.

Eyes wide and fluttering, Monét nodded her head with fear written all over her face. I couldn't blame her because I'd never handled her that way before.

"Get upstairs and do your homework, choose your clothes for tomorrow and then come down here and help me finish getting dinner on the table. One thing I refuse to have in my house is someone I gave birth to getting smart with me. You're excused!"

Monét ran up to her room and I sat down in the nearest kitchen chair to evaluate what had just happened. I'd never talked back to my parents, not ever…and my parents didn't have to spank me so I didn't spank mine, but my daughter was close to getting a switch on her behind.

Gary had left her a letter that I held on to thinking that she was too young to understand what he might have written, but perhaps he could reach her through his words. Surely had he been here, his little baby girl would not have tried me like she did. Monét hated for her father to be disappointed in her and lived for his approval.

When I walked into Monét's room to hand her the letter, she grabbed me and hugged me tight with tears sliding down her cheeks. She didn't have to say a word because I knew that was her way of apologizing. I returned her hug and handed her the letter before I changed my mind and left her to read words her father had written just for his baby girl. Lord, I pray her daddy's words are enough.

Chapter Twenty-Seven

GARY JR.

"Heeeeeeey...can I come in?"

There was no way I was letting this chick into my dorm room. I shouldn't have answered the door. The look on my face should have told her I wasn't pleased with her visit, but she just stood there twisting her hair around her finger trying to look all sweet. Erica the wacko.

"So you're really not going to let me in?"

"Leave...I'm only going to tell you once."

"Heard you're single now, so uh, we can do what we started before...brought my flavas, a little something to smoke and get our drink on," Erica continued as if I didn't say a word.

Peeking my head out into the dorm suite to see if anyone was there, I found a few of my dorm mates sitting on the sofa playing video games.

"Yo, fellas, I told this jump off to leave. She ever come back, don't let her in here." I landed a deadly look at Erica hoping she got the message and just left, but no, she had to try and take me there.

"I got your jump off, yeah, I got it," Erica threatened as she attempted to lunge at me, but I blocked her efforts and held her back by her forehead.

It was impossible for her to land a hit so she started screaming, cursing and jumping, trying to get away from me so she could get at me. Next thing I know, there was a hard knock on the door and I thought it might have been the student advisor. Was I ever wrong; it was other students who resided in dorm suites nearby. A few girls and a couple of my team mates became our spectators as Erica made a fool of herself and I wished her away from me.

When I couldn't get her to calm down, I picked her up and tried to physically remove her from the suite, but when we got close to the door, she put her feet against the wall and resisted, so I dropped her and she landed on the floor with a hard thud.

"Who is talking to this trick?" One girl asked, turning her lips and nose up at Erica.

"Yeah, right," said another girl. "Always trying to get with somebody, ain't nothing but a t.h.o.t. with her stank…"

"You don't even know me, so shut your mouth before I go in it!" Erica confronted the last girl.

"Oh, you ain't sayin' nothing," the girl told her, taking her earrings off and handing them to one of the other girls without ever turning her back.

"No! No, y'all not fighting in here," I attempted to say, but Erica had already jumped on the girl that took her earrings off and the fight ensued.

Hair pulling, punching, scratching, yelling, instigating and anything else that could fuel a fight moved with a frenzy. The crowd grew bigger and the yelling became louder with folks rooting for the girl that took off her earrings, whose name happened to be Tasha. I was frozen in my steps because I'd never seen an all-out brawl like that in my life.

When somebody finally had the mind to break it up, our resident advisor and a few security guards were in the dorm suite sending students back to their dorms and pulling Erica and Tasha apart. I retreated to my room so that I would not be implicated in the melee.

Shortly after there was a strong knock on my door and my heart filled with dread. I already knew they were going to kick me out along with the girls because they would say I started it.

"Gary Simmons," the security guard said my name when I opened my door, "Step out here please."

The girls were still there and had given their account of what happened as to why they were fighting in a suite they had no business in unless they were invited. I didn't want to look at either one of them because I didn't want my name involved. Moms is going to be livid and I'm not trying to do her any more harm.

The resident advisor asked me to tell them what happened as to why the girls were fighting. The tall nerdy looking guy looked down at me through his glasses as if he blamed me for the fight and any other infraction that may have occurred that day. I started to tell them I had nothing to do with it, but I recited my version hoping I would get away clean.

"Man, this chick...I mean, this girl," I started to explain as I pointed to Erica, "came to my room uninvited. I immediately told her to leave and then I told my boys, John and Drew, that if she ever came back here not to let her in. Then um...Erica got mad because I called her a jump off because she came here offering her body to me..."

"That's a lie!"

"Continue," Nerd dude told me as if Erica didn't have an outburst.

"Then Erica jumped at me and I held her back by her forehead so she couldn't hit me, and she was screaming and yelling trying to get at me. So then, um, I decided I was done with all that noise and physically picked her up to escort her out of the suite, and then um...when we got to the door, she stuck her feet out against the wall so I couldn't move her."

"He's lying and y'all just gonna let him make up a story?" Erica started crying real tears.

"Continue," the resident advisor told me without answering Erica or looking at me; he just kept writing in his pad.

"Since she wanted to resist me, I let her go and she fell on the floor...at some point Tasha here came in and got into an argument with Erica. I told them not to fight in here, but it was like they didn't hear me. Next thing I know, Erica jumped on Tasha and well...that's it."

"Part of your story corroborates with Tasha's story so I tend to believe you. However, I will get back to you to let you three know what will happen from here. You're free to go and I advise you to stay close to your emails, and there will be a formal letter issued to confirm what will be done."

I breathed a sigh of relief for the moment, but two days later all three of us had to stand before a panel in the Student Center that consisted of the Dean of Schools, the RA, and three other faculty members that I did not know. Man, my knees were knocking into each other because I had no idea which way things would go.

"I've read the report thoroughly and looked at each of your records and we have agreed upon the discipline for all three of you. Before I tell you what has been decided, I will give all three of you an opportunity to speak for yourselves so that we can determine if indeed we have made the right decision," the dean told us in her no-nonsense voice.

Erica started first and lied through all of her teeth! I was seething with anger and had to take several deep breaths to keep myself calm. I thought Tasha was going to jump on her right in front of the panel, but she kept balling and releasing both fists while Erica was talking. Why they allowed her to go first was lost on me. When it was Tasha's turn, the cool demeanor that she suddenly took on scared me. I listened intently while she recounted her version of what happened.

"So when I called her a t.h.o.t., she got mad and started coming at me, so I took my earrings off and the next thing I know, she jumps on me. I had to defend myself, Dean."

"I can never keep up with young folks slang...can you tell us what 't.h.o.t.' means?"

"Oh," Tasha chuckled, "It means 'that hoe over there.'"

The Dean visibly raised her eyebrows and one of the faculty members was laughing under his breath, evidenced by his shoulders they shook silently. I wanted to find it funny myself, but I wasn't going to take any chances with the Dean, especially when she leveled her gaze at me. Automatically I just knew I was going home.

"Mr. Gary Simmons...Jr. Tell me your version please."

Starting from the beginning, I recounted the story and prayed that I would not be suspended from school at the same time. Not one word was changed from what I told the RA the night the fight happened. Still, once I finished rehearsing the words to the panel, I felt guilty like I was totally at fault.

"All of you have a seat while I confer with the panel and we will give you our final findings shortly," the Dean told us.

Finally after what felt like forever, the Dean told each of us to come and stand before the panel to learn our fate.

"I'm going to start with you Mr. Simmons...after checking your record and inquiring with your professors and football coaches, you are not a trouble maker. I see you have improved your G.P.A. as well; these things work in your favor. Additionally, I believe every word of your account you gave today as to what took place because it is almost verbatim with the written report I received from the resident advisor. With that said, I am not going to issue any discipline at this time; however, if you ever encounter an uninvited guest, feel free to call security. Continue the good work with your classes and I look forward to witnessing you walk across the stage to receive your Bachelor's degree in two years. You may be seated."

I hurried to the seat I'd just vacated remembering to thank God for the bullet I just dodged. The last thing I wanted to do was to be sent home on suspension and my mother be hurt by something else foolish I'd done. Whew! It was over!

Tasha didn't make out so bad, but because she actually engaged in a fight with Erica when she could have simply kept her mouth shut and remained a spectator, the Dean suspended her for a week. That meant she had to leave the dorm and go home.

Erica started to complain about the Dean's decision concerning Tasha, but was told to keep her comments to herself until she had been told what disciplinary action brought against her.

"Young lady, this is not the first time this panel has seen you in the three years you have been here. Looking through your file, I see that you had an incident where you were disruptive in class and the teacher felt it was in your best interest and the students in the class for you to be dropped. Fortunately you were able to find an equivalent to meet that core class that year. Soon thereafter, you along with some friends started a disturbance in the cafeteria that earned you a week of suspension. Your G.P.A. is not the greatest, but it does not change my mind about the fact that you not only lied to the resident advisor the day of this last incident, you lied again here today. Unacceptable!

"You had no business trying to stay in Mr. Simmons' dorm suite when he asked you to leave, you had no right to physically attack him. I agree he should not have called you a derogatory name; however, you should have taken your leave immediately as requested.

"Finally, your attack on Tasha Jones should not have happened had you left as requested by Mr. Simmons. Students would not have gathered expecting the impending fight that indeed did happen because you attacked first. With that said, Erica Whitaker, you are suspended for one year…"

"What? Uh uh, wait a minute, hold up! Y'all just gonna kick me out for a whole year when I really didn't start this? I'mma get my lawyer, that's what I'm gonna do," Erica twisted her neck and put her hands on her hips. "Phssssst, *please*! There are other schools I can enroll in, I don't have to go here!"

"Your record speaks for itself, Erica. I encourage you to take self-inventory on your time off from school and work on improving yourself and your attitude."

"Yeah, yeah, right, whatever!" was her reply as she made haste to the doors, swinging them open as hard as she could. "My name is Erica, I ain't ever gotta do nothing I don't want to do."

The Dean just sadly shook her head, asked security to make sure she packed and vacated the premises as soon as possible. She then admonished Tasha and me both to keep our noses clean or the same thing would happen to us. A shudder went through me at the very thought of being kicked out of school for a year.

Chapter Twenty-Eight

TONYA

The holidays had come and gone, and we were approaching the one-year anniversary of Gary's passing. I have to admit that I was a lot better than I had been after my father took time to talk to me, but my heart was still so sad. There were days that I would cry for hours missing my husband; I just couldn't help it. But I knew that I had to get my act together because I couldn't live the rest of my life dealing with more than a few bouts of depression. Medication was out of the question even though my doctor prescribed an antidepressant for me. Perhaps I just wanted to feel it, not really sure.

Yes, I made up my mind that it was time that I stepped back into life and live each day like it's my last. My husband isn't coming back, but the love we shared together and the love that created our three children is still here with me. Yet, it was hard to pull it together some days.

Gerald told me that he was definitely going to come home for the weekend because I'd purchased Gary's headstone and I wanted to see it at the cemetery. I approved it when the order came in, but I want my children and my mother-in-law to take a moment and remember my husband in a special way on the first anniversary of his passing. I wasn't too sure Gary Jr. was going to make it since he didn't reply to my text, but I was glad when I heard him come in the house through the kitchen.

"Hey, Ma! What's for dinner?"

"You better get in here and give me a hug and a kiss. You're not too grown for that," I yelled to my oldest son.

"You're looking good, Ma," Gary Jr. told me after he released me from a strong hug. "You good?"

"I'm good, Honey. Your mom is getting better every day."

Which was true, but why tell my son that I still have my moments when I snot and cry all day and refuse to get out of the bed while I open the large plastic bag under my pillow so I can smell my husband and imagine his presence with me. No, this weekend is going to be a good one with great memories of a true man of God. That would be my husband, Mr. Gary Simmons, Sr.

"I don't see no pots jumping in the kitchen; are we going out or something?"

"Going to your Nana Cee's house for dinner, so go up and get situated and then tell your sister we'll be leaving in about 15 minutes."

Gary went upstairs and the next thing I knew, he was running back down the stairs.

"Ma? Ma!"

"What in the world…"

"You know you're gonna have to keep an eye on Monét, I mean, not that you're not, but…when did she get that height on her? And that…that body? That is not my little sister up those stairs," Gary Jr. shook his head. "Can't be!"

I couldn't help but to laugh…it's true that Monét really began to blossom right after the holidays ended and had the nerve to grow another cup size. She is now a 38-DD and I have to admit that I was definitely worried about her and prayed she wouldn't get any bigger because I've never had a bra custom made.

"Your sister is growing up, that's what happened to her," I was so tickled.

"Mom, she's getting…man, I hate to say this, but she's getting…pretty…yuck! I'mma have to hurt these knuckleheads around here because they're going to try to get at her. I'll drive all the way back home too, I'm not playing."

"I don't know why he's trippin', I'm a teenager now, thank you very much. Besides, I ain't into boys, just my books," Monét informed her brother as she walked into the den.

"You heard what I said upstairs, you're growing up too fast!" Gary told his sister, completely frustrated.

Monét and I looked at each other and cracked up laughing at Gary Jr.; he's going to be worse than his father ever would have been.

"Go up and tell Gerald it's time to go over to your grandmother's house. We're all driving over together in my car," I told my son as he started up the stairs still trying to shake off the shock of seeing his sister becoming a young lady.

The ride over sounded the way our family always did with the guys teasing Monét, threatening her and telling her what to do, and Monét letting them know she could do whatever she wanted that I would let her do. The sounds of family is something that is irreplaceable. What am I going to do when they are all grown up and I'm in that big house by myself?

The familial chatter continued at Cecelia's house around the table as we laughed and enjoyed ourselves. It was like a salve to my soul hearing the joy in my children's voices while they shared what they'd been up to in school and with friends. Sounded like they were progressing and working through the grief of losing their father better than I was although sometimes I do worry about my firstborn. When Cecelia asked him if he was still involved with that 'little tramp,' his face clouded over momentarily, but he quickly recovered.

"Nah, Nana Cee, you were right about her. I've seen in her in passing because she lives down the street, but I haven't spoken to her since uh, that time we were here. Before you ask, there's no one else. I actually buckled down this last semester and my grades are good...for me," Gary Jr. laughed and we joined him.

"What about you, Gerald?" I just had to see what my second-born son was up to with girls.

"Mom, you already know, I'm taking my time with my

friend. We're good."

"How good?" Monét asked before anyone else could.

"None of your business, pest! Just make sure I don't have to chase none of those little knuckleheads away from you or..."

"Or what? I ain't thinking about none those big head boys. Dana's the one doing that..." Monét's voice trailed off.

"Is that right," her grandmother asked her as she wiped the corners of her mouth. "So what exactly is it that Dana is doing?"

"Aw, Nana Cee, you know," Monét whined. "She does things with them..."

"You better not be doing anything with them, you best believe *that*," Gary Jr. threatened. "I should transfer to a school closer to home so I can come pick you up from school 'cause I don't want to have to hurt nobody."

"Hush, wait a minute, let me finish talking to Sweat Pea... now you need to tell me what exactly Dana is doing with these boys because I don't want you to end up doing something too."

"No way! Dana is nasty! She's already having sex and I've been kind of, you know, not hanging with her."

I'd noticed Dana's visits to our house had started to wane and Monét was spending more time with Dawn, but I didn't really question it because friendships can go in cycles sometimes. Had I known what Monét was sharing with us at the dinner table, I would have shut it all down for her.

"She's not welcome back in our house," Gary Jr. stated as if he made the decisions in our home.

"Oh boy, bye!" Monét rolled her eyes. "You're not the boss of me."

"What else is there you're not telling us, Sweet Pea?" Cecelia insisted, ignoring the confrontation between Monét and Gary Jr. "There is something else, isn't there?"

"Nana Cee, you don't miss nothing, do you? Okay...Dana's pregnant and her mother is going to let her stay with her grandmother until the baby is born. That's the other reason why Dana hasn't been over...her mother said she's embarrassed."

"Well, if she lets her wear all kinds of sexy undergarments and pretty much do what she wants to do..." I started to say.

"Not really, Mom; she was sneaking and doing most of what she did and that's why she can't be a close friend any more. I don't want to be friends with someone who doesn't care about themselves. We learned about safe sex in school and she still didn't make sure the boys she slept with used protection."

My mother-in-law and I exchanged glances and then I allowed her to take over the conversation.

"Listen to me real good, Monét; you did the right thing. Not that she can't be a friend, but the other boys will start thinking you're the same type of girl when you're not. It will cause you more problems than you are able to deal with. Now you said boys, meaning more than one boy Dana was sleeping with?"

"Yes, Nana Cee, and she didn't care. That's why I was mad with her for a while. Just nasty! Now she's not even sure who the father is. She should be embarrassed not her mother. Her Mom had to work long hours and expected Dana to pitch in and help with her siblings, but she was too busy sneaking boys in the house having sex to even worry about them. I'm disappointed because we always talked about what we were going to do when we grow up and now our plans are ruined."

"Your plans are not ruined," Gerald told his sister with a sympathetic look on his face. "Little Sis, whatever your dreams and goals are, continue to pursue them for yourself with God's help. You don't need anybody other than the people He puts in your life to help you reach them. Okay, pest?"

"You make me sick, Gerald! Yes, I hear you," my daughter smiled at her brother, but I noticed Gary sat with his arms crossed with nothing to say.

~~~~~~~~

The following day we went to Gary's grave at the cemetery, something I felt we should do to remember him a full year after his passing. It was so hard to look at that headstone and see my husband's name, date of birth and death, and the inscription, *Beloved husband, father and son.* I should have had them put, 'Tonya's Heart.' It was buried six feet under the earth with my husband…or maybe he took it with him to heaven.

Monét sat down on the ground in front of the headstone and placed three white roses in front of it and traced every letter with her finger. She did it over and over again until she broke down crying, saying she wanted her Daddy back. My heart ached as I lowered myself to hold her in my arms and rock her as she kept telling me she wanted her father. We all cried hard, but one by one we each shared something about Gary that brought us joy. Gerald summed everything up by saying, "I will always remember how committed Dad was to everything he involved himself with…and the fact that He loved God enough to prepare his family for his passing on so many levels. I'm sad he's no longer with us, but I am equally as happy that we were blessed to have him in our lives."

When Gerald finished talking, we stood silently for a few more minutes before we headed back to our cars. Gary Jr. lingered a little longer. He laid both hands on the headstone and cried, his body trembled with his pent up grief. I started to go back to him, but Gerald assured me he would stay with his brother and suggested the rest of us go back to the house.

"We'll be there shortly, Mom. That's why I drove," Gerald smiled. He's more like Gary Sr. than I realized before today.

It was a long drive back to the house because the following day was Sunday, and it will be a year to the day that Gary passed away. I'm sure there will be a few church members who are going to remember and I'm not certain if I'm up to anybody acknowledging it openly. No matter. I promised my father, myself and God that I was going to actively join in the grieving process so I can get through it. No better time than the present.

Sunday morning was calm as we all prepared ourselves for church after a hearty breakfast I decided to cook at the last minute. Deciding that it was time to wash the sheets that Gary last laid upon forced me to the basement at 6 a.m. that morning, so I had to keep doing something with my hands after I'd gotten dressed. The day had come that I was going to take the first step to cherishing my husband's memory and dealing with the grief that was my private anguish day in and day out.

Will I always feel this way? I'm sure I won't, but I couldn't really call it at that point…there are times I hurt like Gary just passed away, and there are times I can vividly remember something we shared that would bring me so much joy. The ups and the downs were so sharp until sometimes I didn't know whether I was coming or going. But this day, I chose to go...forward, that is. Honor my husband's memory and be the best mother to our children I can possibly be, never forgetting him and urging my children to do the same thing.

Breakfast was uneventful with the exception of Gerald and Monét going at it, something that would normally include Gary Jr. He pushed his breakfast around his plate and tuned us out as if we were not sitting at the same table.

"Gary, what's wrong?"

"Huh? Oh...nothing, Ma. I'm not all that hungry."

"Can I have your bacon then?" Monét reached over Gerald and grabbed a few pieces from Gary's plate. That would have been a fight any other day. Instead, Gary Jr. excused himself and headed up to his room.

"We're leaving in 30 minutes!" I yelled after him.

"Can I drive your car, Mom? Makes no sense for us to go to the same place in different cars," Gerald volunteered.

"I don't mind. Do you know what's wrong with your brother?"

"Pretty much he's still having a hard time dealing with Dad not being here. G won't admit it, but he's really messed up."

"We've got to pray especially for him," I patted Gerald's hand. "Well, let me clean these dishes so we will be on time for service."

"Pest, help Mom clean the kitchen."

"Mom didn't tell me I had to..."

"That's a good idea. Monét help me clear the dishes and wash the table off. I'll take care of the dishes," I told my disappointed daughter.

"Ugggggghhhhhh, you make me *sick*!" she said to Gerald, but Monét's words were really for me. I let her slide this time.

Kitchen cleaned, last minute preparations taken care of and we were on our way. I prayed for my oldest son that God would touch his heart today and help him come to terms with his father's death. I've been so busy wallowing in my pain that I had not paid too much attention to how my children were coping with the loss. Being the oldest and the namesake was a special thing to Gary Jr., and he's always lived to show his father that he was the person we raised him to be. Today is definitely a good day for me to pull myself together and deal with me so I can help my children as well.

Worship service was starting when we walked through the doors, and it didn't take long for it to get heated. I love music and our church's praise team has always been a wonderful ministry, uplifting members preparing them for the rest of the service. Singing has been so much a part of me for my entire life that no matter what, if I can simply listen to a song that glorifies God, I can leave my slump if only for a little while.

The surprise of the service is when Monét walked up to the mic to lead the sermonic selection. The youth choir was singing, and Nicole, the young lady I mentored years ago, was still in charge of the choir. She's married now with two children of her own and still in love with the youth choir. I couldn't keep my seat when the music to Gary's favorite song started to play and Nicole took another mic to talk to the congregation.

"Praise the Lord everybody!" she shouted joyously and waited for the congregation to respond. "Today is a special day for Monét and the Simmons family because it marks the one-year anniversary of the passing of Deacon Gary Simmons, Sr. Now most of you know Monét would never lead a song although I've always known she has a beautiful voice *like her momma*. Everybody laughed and I joined them. "So you know I couldn't turn this baby down when she asked if we could sing her dad's favorite song and allow her to lead it. I want y'all to get with her now, and stand on your feet and let the Lord bless you real good."

When the organist played the opening notes for "God Is," the choir started the song, which was a different arrangement. But as soon as I heard my baby come in on the lead vocals, I nearly jumped out of my seat! Sing like me? Oh no, my baby's voice is beautiful! Monét did not miss a note, and her clear soprano voice had such a soothing sound to it, the anointing evident in the gift God had given her. It wasn't long before the tears were flowing and I was praising God…my baby had come out of her shell!

Gerald was standing beside me supporting his sister while Gary continued to sit, but he was attentive because I'm sure he was shocked since neither of us has ever heard Monét sing this way. Around the house she would practice new songs the choir was singing, but never to lead a song. Next thing I knew, I heard my mother-in-law's voice:

"Sang it, Miss Mo! That's my grandbaby right there! Sing it, Sweet Pea, sing!"

Monét had to tell her grandmother what she was going to do, because she was right there with her loud yellow two-piece suit, matching shoes and big floppy church hat supporting her granddaughter. She had the nerve to come out in the aisle so Monét could see and hear her, but my baby girl kept her focus and never wavered or appeared nervous at all.

When she finished singing the song, with heavy tears flowing down her face, Monét told Gary, "This song is for you, Daddy...I might not have you here with me, but I'll always have your song."

Lord, have mercy! I was no more good. Instead of going back to sit with the choir, Monét decided to sit between Gerald and me after her grandmother almost hugged the breath out of her. Gary smiled at her and hugged her too, which was a surprise as well, but a good one. Then before everybody could settle down, Pastor Jackson stood up in the pulpit and greeted us.

"How are you good folks doing on this day, the day that the Lord has made? I tell you what...I know who I'm going to ask to sing solos for me when Tonya can't, praise Jesus. Come to me, Monét, and let me lay hands on you and pray for you... God's anointing is on this child...do you hear me? His anointing is on this child."

After Pastor Jackson prayed for Monét and sent her back to her seat, he took his text and also acknowledged the passing of my husband. He also recognized Gary's mother and thanked her for joining us this morning and went on into his message.

"For those of you who need a topic, I have one for you... "Change Me for My Season." Now don't look at me like I'm trying to be super-duper deep with you like some folks do when they talk about one season or another like they know what God is doing in a particular season."

My pastor has put on quite a few pounds over the years, so it didn't take him long into the message to start mopping his brow with a white hand towel and reach over to take a sip of water before he continued. After he'd read into our hearing Romans 12:2, he went a little further.

"Sometimes flesh ain't ready to meet the challenge or situation, but we must push beyond our flesh to victory in God. Through meeting God by getting in his face, we can say: "I'm ready, let's go; I'm ready to get through this, hallelujah!" Cause you see, there are situations in our life that we are living in that we are not ready to face, don't want to face, yet we are living in them...the death of a loved one, a daughter pregnant too young and out of wedlock, a son or daughter locked up, the loss of a job held for years...whatever the situation might be that we can't seem to wrap our hearts and minds around, God is the One Who has to change how we think through His Word. By staying in God's Word, He will help us in our spirits as well. Yes, ladies and gentlemen, if we go to God with it, we will come out all right!

Pastor Jackson's message was punctuated with plenty of 'amens,' and 'I know that's right, Pastor!' and some 'hallelujah's' too. But as I listened quietly, something began to open up in my heart and the place I was working hard not to get to was in my view. Total acceptance and peace in spite of my loss.

"See, what I believe happens is the very thing that goes on with a butterfly." Pastor Jackson kept going. "We see a beautiful butterfly flitting around looking all good, but I'm sure there was a story that could have been told inside of that cocoon. When you understand the process the butterfly goes through from the caterpillar to the cocoon to the butterfly, you will see that a transformation took place in there. For us, we bury ourselves in God's Word and allow HIM to transform us by renewing our minds. That is when we are able to get in God's face with whatever it is and allow Him to change us for the season we are living in. Do you hear me in here, praise Jesus!

"Now listen to me saints, about "seasons"...don't make

more of the notion of "seasons" than God intended. As reflected in God's Word, "season/seasons" is a word simply intended to reflect ...a change in circumstances, situations or conditions. I want you to take some time this week and read the scripture from my text and Ecclesiastes 3:1-8 in case you don't get the gist of this message, maybe it will catch you as you go," Pastor chuckled.

"Though *natural* 'season(s)' may remain intact for predictable and extended periods of time, we CAN NOT expect the same of God's 'seasons' in our lives. God is not bound by time. With Him a season may last years, months, weeks, days, or...just a few moments.

"Just be assured of this: Various "seasons" *will come*...and they will *go*. Expect nothing of this life to sustain itself forever, but trust GOD to sustain YOU!"

Pastor Jackson wasn't as longwinded as he used to be, but there was no doubt that the message touched many hearts. Before he made the altar call, Pastor called for my family to come first so he could pray for us. It had been a rough year, but we were doing our best to look to God to continue to carry us through.

Chapter Twenty-Eight

TONYA
One year later…

Gary's been gone for two years now and things have improved so much for the Simmons family. I finally got around to redecorating my formal living room with Lisa doing most of the work. My friend knows she can put something together that looks like it cost an arm and a leg, but it is beautiful! All of that work and I still don't want anyone sitting in my living room. Lisa said I'd better figure something out because she didn't put in her time and my money for nothing.

I'm proud of her taking the initiative to open her own shop in our hometown, "Lisa's Designs." She's not worried about trying to make a whole lot of money since her divorce settlement was rather hefty along with the child support her ex-husband has to pay. Her clients from California were able to stay in touch with her, so she still catered to them the best she could from the new location. Lisa and Brian were also able to work out visitation for the children, with Dawn spending most of her time with Lisa and BJ with his father, his girlfriend and his new son. As much as I wanted my friend's marriage to work, I had to agree the baby was a deal breaker.

Denise, Denise, Denise...I love that girl! Having a baby at 45 changed her in ways I never thought I would witness. The Lord really blessed little Nia Solange to pull through and she is a healthy little two year-old with those golden colored eyes. Denise wants to let her model but I don't know if that's a good idea, especially since Nia's father decided he could not deny she was his and decided to be a man and take care of his daughter. I told Denise she'd better not slip up and get back with that man to give Nia a sibling, and she told me to stop cussing at her. I'm proud of her though...she changed churches and decided she'd played Russian roulette with her life and games with God long enough. It was time to get real.

My sons are now juniors in college pursuing their educational goals, but what surprised me is they didn't want to try to go further professionally with sports. They loved playing basketball with Gary since they were little boys, but Gary found football to be his favorite and he played well. I'm proud of them both...Gerald followed in his father's footsteps in more ways than one, and Gary Jr. talked about going into the education field and working his way up to the position of principal. If it is true that our loved ones are looking down on us, Gary Simmons Sr. is up in heaven looking down here, grinning from ear-to-ear and bragging to anyone who would listen about his twin sons that look like him.

Don't get him started on his baby girl...she's started her first year of high school and is holding her own with her grades. Monét hasn't decided exactly what she wants to do with her life yet, but singing is not a priority.

"Mom, I only led one song and everybody wants me to *siiiiiing*," she whined one afternoon. "I am *not* little Tonya Henderson. Doesn't most of our church members know you married Daddy and you're a Simmons?"

I had to laugh because she's right; I don't want anyone to compare her to me, just allow her to come into her own. She's doing a pretty good job of that, and I am just as proud of her as I am of my sons. Monét even helped me go through her father's things so I could decide what I was giving away, and what I was going to keep. It wasn't an easy task since some of his clothing had his favorite cologne lingering on them. At least I was able to save my tears until I was alone because there are still times I miss that man to the core of my soul.

Out of my three children, Gary Jr. is the one I'm most worried about because I don't believe he has totally come to terms with losing his father. He still has bouts of depression when he'd rather stay to himself, not eat or hang out with his friends. Then he will flip and be his normal joking self, laughing and fooling around. My prayer is the times he's quiet is for reflection and strength because he always tell me he's fine, nothing's wrong. My Dad decided he'd keep in closer touch with Gary Jr. in the event he is ready to open up and share his heart.

One thing certainly changed after all my friends and I have been through, and that is our commitment to keep up with each other better. Sometimes Lisa would stop by with Dawn on her way home from the shop so we would Skype with Denise, or we would all set a time from each of our homes to catch up on things. We were online one evening and Denise made it clear that she needed a real vacation.

"This little girl exhausts me, do you hear me? She wants me to play with her toys after I've worked all day...I've got to find just a little piece of peace for at least a long weekend. It might not be so bad if her first word wasn't her almost was a deadbeat daddy," Denise complained.

"Don't get mad at that precious little baby because you can't keep up with her with your old self," Lisa laughed.

"Old? Honey, let me tell you something about me...the young guys are still inquiring, but uh, I ain't got time to be playing with no kids," we all laughed.

"Do you have any idea where you'd like to go on vacation, either of you?" I asked.

"Where is that place you mentioned some time ago before Gary got sick...some kind of island or something?"

"Right, Lisa! Gary and I were sitting on deck before the cruise ship pulled out in Miami and you could look over and see these beautiful mansions, and there is a beach and everything. I can check into it and find out pricing if we can agree on when we'd like to go."

"Tomorrow," Denise deadpanned. "Do you see these gray soldiers starting to march through my hair? That means now is not too late to run for the island."

"Girl, just still crazy as all get out. Why don't we wait until the kids get out of school? That way I know that Dawn will be with her father and BJ can wait another week or so to visit with me," Lisa suggested.

"I'm okay with that...my guys will be home from school and Monét can stay with my parents or Cecelia...it's on you, Denise, what say you?"

"I already told you what I say, but since you want to wait until the end of school, I guess I can hang on until then. In the event that I lose my mind and find a way to go without y'all, don't get mad, hear?" That's when we heard a crash and a yell coming from Denise's end. "Nia! I've got to go, ladies. Let me know the date so I can get the time off from work and Nia. She will be spending that long weekend with her grandmother. 'Nighty-night!"

Denise signed off and Lisa and I worked online together to find out what Star Island had to offer and what we could get into while we were there. I was looking forward to the pretty sand of the beach, the feel of the ocean water on my feet and the breeze blowing through my hair.

One week after school was out for Monét, my friends and I caught a flight straight to Miami, rented a car and headed to Star Island. It turns out that the best we could do is tour the island because it is a highly exclusive neighborhood in South Beach. We booked a tour because I had to see the beautiful homes and the beaches. Truth be told, I wanted to sell my house and move there, but who am I fooling? There is no way I could live that far away from family and friends.

Since our plans changed to Treasure Island, we drove to Kissimmee, Florida and rented a condo on the beach that included a full kitchen in case we decided we wanted to buy food and cook while we were there. Right, as if that would happen. We dined out every day and enjoyed the beach and ocean. It was beautiful! Such a relaxing trip, something I didn't realize how badly we all needed it until we arrived. Being near the ocean was such a freeing experience that I considered taking more than one trip a year to this location.

Seven whole days of freedom and time to reflect on so many things, especially the past two years or so. I never thought I would be a widow! Finally able to fill out important papers and not feel shaky inside when I checked the box that says, 'widow.' Gary and I married right out of college after so much tug of war and back and forth between us. He pursued me and there were times when my heart yearned for him and it seemed he didn't want me, but I wasn't going to let him know it. It was like our love had to fight to right itself, but when we got into our own groove, it was a beautiful love. We felt each other without being present, and we loved from a place that only a few experience. I know that I married the man God wanted me to marry, but I still find myself questioning why He took him from me so soon.

Each day we decided on something different, even a trip to Disney and just enjoying one another's company. The beach, swimming (I put my feet in the water because I can't swim), beautiful and expensive restaurants, shopping until we dropped and just relaxing took up our time. Reminded me of when we were growing up and we were determined to find something to do to keep us occupied while we tried to hurry and grow up. Now that we're grown, the best we can do is treasure our memories and make new ones together.

Poor Denise, she missed Nia something terrible and called her mother several times a day, driving her crazy. Most of her conversation the whole trip was about her precious baby girl, and Lisa made no bones about telling her we didn't get away from our children to talk about them the entire time. "Shoot, we could have stayed home with them if all we're going to do is talk about them," she complained.

The last day of our trip, we were laying out on beach chairs as close as we could get to the ocean when I decided to walk off the seafood dinner we had. As soon as I got up, Lisa wanted to know if she could come along.

"Not this time," I told her as I grabbed my cell phone. "Just walking and thinking…I'll be back shortly."

Before going home, I wanted to reflect on this last week and the last two years of my life without my husband, so I slipped my ear buds on and listened to the first track of music that came up. Marvin Sapp's song, "My Testimony" started playing immediately and I walked slowly savoring each and every word, realizing his song and testimony was mine as well.

I had sense enough to know that I wasn't the only person to experience such a devastating tragedy in life, and like Marvin said, I made it through. The pain that I used to physically feel in my heart is no longer there, and I have finally been able to clean out most of Gary's things from the bedroom we shared. Every time I would attempt to do it before, I couldn't because it felt like I was removing him permanently as if he'd never been there.

It wasn't until I unpacked the box BAN sent to the house with Gary's things that I was able to set my husband free and cherish him all at the same time. Every family portrait and pictures of the children took me through the years of our union. The love that shone brightly in each one as we grew brought the tears and my heart spilled over with the love we were blessed to create together. Why couldn't I see that before?

So as I continued to walk with my bare feet touching the ocean water, enjoying the sand and breeze across my face and hair, I understood that it was okay to cry because I miss my husband. Or laugh at something I remember he said or did, or smile as I reminisce over the years we spent together…and I don't have to wallow under a cloud of depression to do it.

In the letter my husband left for me, he told me not to allow his absence to cause an empty space in my heart because the love that has been there will be there forever. He asked me not to be angry with him for leaving so soon, and had the nerve to jokingly say not to worry, he trusts me with his children. I still chuckle about that; my husband the jokester.

As I continued to walk and the sun began to set, I whispered to the wind, "Our love forever, Gary…" with a kiss that followed along behind it. I pray God allows him to catch it.

Meet Sharel E. Gordon-Love

Born and raised in Plainfield, New Jersey, Sharel E. Gordon-Love started writing at the age of six, winning immediate recognition for her essays and short stories. Her first nonfiction work, "Is There Hope for the Black Male?" was published by Black Child Magazine in 1994. Certified in Microcomputer Technology and Business Administration, Sharel graduated from Berkeley College of Business in 1993.

Sharel's short story, "I'll Always Be Just a Thought Away," can be found in an anthology compiled by Satchel titled "The HEART of OUR COMMUNITY," in 2006. Her first novel, When He Calls, was released in 2002, followed by The Putting Away in 2011, for which Sharel was nominated for Breakout Author of the Year 2011 by the African American Literary Awards Show. Change Me for My Season, is the third novel in the "Seasons of Life" series.

Founder and CEO of Inspirational Literary Works LLC, as well as an inspirational speaker, Sharel is a licensed evangelist in the Church of God in Christ, and along with her family, attend New Reid Temple C.O.G.I.C. in East Orange, New Jersey. There she serves on the Administrative staff, Youth Department, and Women's Department ministries. Sharel, resides in North Plainfield, New Jersey with her family.

www.ingramcontent.com/pod-product-compliance
Lightning Source LLC
Chambersburg PA
CBHW020557250626
47154CB00004B/1250